מסורה

ArtScroll Youth Series®

The Best of

Compiled from the pages of
Olomeinu
by
Rabbi Yaakov Fruchter

Edited for publication by
Rabbi Nosson Scherman

Illustrated by
Yosef Dershowitz
Designed by
Sheah Brander

BOOK ONE

Olomeinu®
STORIES FOR ALL YEAR 'ROUND

Published by

Mesorah Publications, ltd

in conjunction with
Torah Umesorah
National Society for Hebrew Day Schools

FIRST EDITION
First Impression ... November 1981
Second Impression ... December 1982
Third Impression ... January 1984
Fourth Impression ... May 1987

Published and Distributed by
MESORAH PUBLICATIONS, Ltd.
1969 Coney Island Avenue
Brooklyn, New York 11223

Also available to schools and students through
TORAH UMESORAH PUBLICATIONS
160 Broadway
New York, N.Y. 10038

Distributed in Europe by
J. LEHMANN HEBREW BOOKSELLERS
20 Cambridge Terrace
Gateshead, Tyne and Wear
England NE8 1RP

Typography by CompuScribe at ArtScroll Studios, Ltd.
1969 Coney Island Avenue / Brooklyn, N.Y. 11223 / (212) 339-1700

בס״ד

This first anthology of Torah literature for the young

is dedicated in honor of

Mr. and Mrs. Adolph Beren

of Marietta, Ohio,

and Mr. Harry H. Beren and Mr. Israel H. Beren

of Fort Worth, Texas.

Members of the Beren family,

through their concern for the Torah education of our youth,

have written a significant chapter in the history of the

American Jewish community.

This volume, which will inspire thousands of

Jewish children throughout the world

with the beauty of our heritage,

is indeed a most fitting tribute to their efforts.

TORAH UMESORAH

National Society for Hebrew Day Schools

Kislev 5742

Preface

בס"ד

... בָּא חֲבַקּוּק וְהֶעֱמִידָן עַל אַחַת שֶׁנֶּאֱמַר, וְצַדִּיק בֶּאֱמוּנָתוֹ יִחְיֶה
*The prophet Chavakuk came and established one primary
principle (Makkos 24a): A righteous person must live by his
faith (Chavakuk 2:4).*

It is with a deep sense of gratitude to *Hashem Yisborach* that the Torah
Umesorah Publications Department, together with Mesorah
Publications, publishers of the ArtScroll Series, embark upon this joint
effort in publishing the "Best of Olomeinu" stories in book form. It is
an important event, and we are certain it will be greeted with joy and
enthusiasm by the entire Jewish community.

The OLOMEINU-OUR WORLD childrens magazine, published by
Torah Umesorah, The National Society for Hebrew Day Schools, is now
in its thirty-sixth year of publication. OLOMEINU was a pioneer in
providing Yeshiva-Day School students with unadulterated, enjoyable,
wholesome reading material on Torah subjects, personalities, and
values. In its fourth decade, OLOMEINU continues to fill the tremendous shortage of Torah-true literature for our children, written on their
level, and with which they can identify. OLOMEINU strives to maintain
high literary standards and artistic professionalism, coupled with
scrupulous adherence to the guidelines of the *Shulchan Aruch* and the
insight and guidance of the *Gedolai Yisrael,* whose accolades and
encouragement the magazine has always received. Over a quarter of a
century of readers — children, parents, and grandparents — have been
touched, inspired, warmed, and nurtured along the path of Torah,
mitzvos, and *ma'asim tovim* by the many exciting stories and features
of monthly OLOMEINU issues. It is only natural, therefore, that
OLOMEINU, the trailblazer of reading material *al taharas hakodesh* for
children, join with ArtScroll, the trailblazer of reading material *al*

vi

taharas hakodesh for adults, to produce this anthology of stories for the Jewish community.

OLOMEINU was the dream of Torah Umesorah's founder, Rabbi Shraga Feivel Mendelowitz, זצ״ל, and now it has blossomed into an international publication, with editions appearing in Spanish, French, and German.

The original purpose of this special magazine for children was to help preserve, strengthen — and rekindle, if necessary — the אֱמוּנָה פְּשׁוּטָה (simple faith) inherent in the *neshama* of every Jewish child, through stories of *Gedolim* and other features that foster and breathe a love for Torah and *mitzvos, middos tovos* and *yiras shamayim*, which children can emulate. In addition it had to counteract the torrent of influences alien to Torah that flowed from nearly all juvenile publications. OLOMEINU remains faithful to these goals.

Many individuals over the years have been involved in the process of bringing OLOMEINU to our children, either as editors, writers, artists or supporters. As we begin this new chapter in our history, we take note of some of them.

From the outset, it was people like Rabbis Bernard Goldenberg, the present National Director of Torah Umesorah; Charles Wengrovsky, and the late Alexander S. Gross ע״ה; who later with Dr. Joseph Kaminetsky, National Director Emeritus; and such lay leaders as the Spero, LeVine, Bunim, Feuerstein, Alpert and Sisselman families, with the assistance of the Torah Umesorah staff, shouldered the burden of producing monthly issues.

Throughout the years the magazine was fortunate in having on its staff such capable people as Rabbi Israel Shurin, who has been serving as Hebrew editor almost from its inception; Rabbis Moshe Yechiel Friedman, and Nisson Wolpin who served as editors; and Rabbi Nosson Scherman and Mordechai Weisz, who now serve as editor and art editor respectively; as well as a group of dedicated writers, some of whose masterful stories appear in this book. Mention should be made also of Balshon typesetters and Non Stop lithographers for the dedicated work they did for many years in helping to produce a beautiful product.

The aesthetic beauty of this book and its professional quality is a tribute to Sheah Brander of Mesorah Publications, who designed it and is responsible for its good taste and appearance, to Yosef Dershowitz who illustrated it, as well as to the entire staff of Mesorah Publications, under the leadership of Rabbi Nosson Scherman who edited the stories for publication and Rabbi Meir Zlotowitz, whose attention and supervision helped make this collection a work of excellence.

A special יְיַשֵּׁר כֹּחַ is due to Mr. David M. Singer for giving generously of his time to help initiate this series of anthologies. Thanks also to Rivkie Neuschloss and Nicky Levy of the OLOMEINU and Publications Department of Torah Umesorah for their assistance and dedication, as well as to the other members of the Torah Umesorah staff for their encouragement.

And אַחֲרוֹן אַחֲרוֹן חָבִיב, my sincere appreciation to my wife Nechama תחי' for her devoted efforts in assisting with the compilation of stories for this book, her valuable insights, encouragement, and able assistance throughout the years in helping me produce OLOMEINU regularly, בעזהש"י; as well as to our children יחי' for their suggestions and cooperation, and to my mother תחי', our source of inspiration.

This preface, however, would not be complete without singling out two individuals who, at the most crucial times in the publication's existence, gave unselfishly of their artistic and writing talents to put the magazine on a high level and to make it worthy of the fame and praise it now enjoys: Rabbi Beryl Merling ע"ה and Nachum (Nat) Fruchter ע"ה, who worked under the pseudonym of Anol Amay. יהא זכרם ברוך.

It is the fruits of all the above that we offer you in this first and subsequent anthologies of the "Best of Olomeinu" series.

It is our sincere wish that, in the merit of the אֱמוּנָה פְּשׁוּטָה we strive to strengthen and preserve in our children, we be brought a step closer in our march to greet מָשִׁיחַ צִדְקֵנוּ בִּמְהֵרָה בְיָמֵנוּ.

כ"ח תשרי תשמ"ב

Rabbi Yaakov Fruchter
Managing Editor, Olomeinu/Our World
Director, Torah Umesorah Publications

viii

Table of Contents

The Flame

by Rabbi Leibel Newman

No one knew his secret. No one would ever know. His *rebbi* had sworn him to secrecy and a secret it would remain. Rabbi Shimon was now an old man approaching his seventies. His long flowing beard was already fully white with just a touch of grey here and there. His feet didn't quite spring from the ground as they always had. Yes, Rabbi Shimon was no longer a young man, but, every so often his mind would wander back to that memorable day fifty-seven years before. He remembered it as though it had happened yesterday. He was now the famous rabbi of a large city in Poland and students came from far and wide to sit at his feet in his world famous yeshiva. But with all that he was, and with all that he had, he could never forget *that* day.

Rabbi Shimon had lived as a young boy in a small village in Lithuania. His mother unfortunately had died when he was only three. Scarcely could he remember how she looked. Everyone in the small village had only words of praise for her. They all agreed that she had been a true *tzadekes* (righteous woman).

His health had been very poor when he was young and many a time his father had to stay home from work to care for him. They lived in a small one-room house with just a small table and two chairs as their furniture. For their beds they used the hard floor covered with a little straw. That was all they could afford. His father worked very hard, but the money he earned was barely enough to pay for Shimon's tuition and the little family's food.

Reb Yosef, his *rebbi,* was the only outstanding Torah scholar in the village. He taught all the children of the little village. Most of them, however, only stayed until they knew how to learn *Chumash* on their own. After that they had to help their fathers at work and there was no time for learning. Some children, whose fathers were a little richer, even stayed for *Mishnayos* and one or two even for *Gemara.* All the children, both young and old, loved Reb Yosef and Reb Yosef loved them.

Shimon's father was not rich but he wanted his son to grow up to be a true *talmid chacham* (Torah scholar). This was his only wish in life and it was what his late wife of blessed memory had always wanted from their only son. Even if it meant that he had to work until late at night, he was going to make sure that Shimon would be a real *talmid chacham.*

Life in the village had been very peaceful, but a savage man by the name of Bogdon Chmielnitzki wouldn't let it stay that way. Chmielnitzki was the wicked leader of the Cossacks. He had joined forces with the Crimean Tartars to fight against the Polish king. His forces far outnumbered the Poles and routed them in a short time. His bands invaded every city and village in their path. Even more than he hated the Poles, Chmielnitzki hated the Jews, and it was the Jews who suffered the most. Jewish blood flowed freely over the brown earth of Poland as the Cossacks killed and burned all in their path.

Shimon's village was not far from Pinsk, a city the Cossacks were very eager to take, and the people knew that their days were numbered. It would not be long until they also would be overrun by those ruthless murderers.

Reb Yosef was the center of attention. Everyone ran to their only *talmid chacham* for advice. What should they do. What *could* they do?

Reb Yosef's kind face strained with the troubles of his fellow villagers as he advised them.

"Yaakov Avinu was faced with a problem very similar to ours when he was about to meet his brother Esav. How did he prepare himself? The Torah tells us that he did three things. First, he prepared a beautiful present to pacify his brother. Second, he prayed to Hashem to save him from the clutches of the wicked Esav. Finally, he readied himself for war.

"Presents will not help with the Cossacks; they are too wild and are out to murder. We are left with the remaining two alternatives — prayer and war. First we must pray to Hashem. All of us must take upon ourselves a day of fasting and devote that entire period to return to Hashem with all our heart and soul. Maybe Hashem will have mercy on us. Then we must be prepared to fight and fight until our last man. If we try our best Hashem will help us."

"Are we prepared?," asked Reb Yosef.

"Yes!" was the resounding reply heard from the lips of all the villagers.

The very next day the streets were unusually quiet. The familiar creaking of old doors could not be heard. The regular hustle and bustle on Main Street was missing. Where was everyone?

A look into the shul would have answered the question. Not a seat was empty. Even the aisles were packed with people. A respectful silence filled the synagogue. The old Reb Yosef was speaking. A sincere feeling of *Teshuva* was descending upon everyone present. Tears could be seen moving down even the small red cheeks of the little children. Everyone knew that this might very well be the last time that they would all be together, but a true faith in Hashem was in everyone's heart. Hashem would not forsake them.

Night came and the fast was over. It was now time for the men to begin preparing themselves for a battle they knew little how to fight. Only one of the villagers, Reb Asher, had ever been in the army. He was given command of all the men. The women and children were ordered to stay home and hide in the cellars.

Reb Asher, the "general," knew that their only chance against the well-armed Cossacks was a surprise attack. He planned to have his men hide in the thick green bushes that surrounded the village until the Cossacks passed by. Then they would attack from behind and hopefully, with Hashem's help, rout them.

Even though most of the boys of Shimon's age were allowed to go along with the men, he was one of the "weaklings" who were told to stay home. Shimon didn't want to remain behind but he knew that he must obey. Sadly he went to the brown wooden cupboard in his room and took out a thick wax candle. Next Shimon went to the closet where his *seforim* (Hebrew books) were kept and took out his torn *Gemara*. Books were expensive in those days and not many people owned a *Gemara* in this village. He, thank G-d, was one of the few that had this great *zechus* (privilege).

Slowly he stepped down into the cold black cellar. It wasn't much more than a pit with a little lime on the walls. He lit the candle and carefully opened his dearest possession. A few moments later all his troubles were forgotten and the sweet beautiful *Gemara nigun* (tune) was heard from his pale lips.

The Cossacks were on the move. Village after village fell to the cruel murderers. The advance troops of the Cossacks were already approaching Shimon's unfortunate village. Little did they know what was lying in wait for them behind those thick bushes. The Cossack leader with his lieutenants was leading the advance party. Just a few feet now separated them from Reb Asher and his men. Even the harsh panting of the horses could be clearly heard by the villagers waiting in ambush.

Suddenly, the Cossack leader let out a yell. His men quickly halted their horses.

"There is something strange about this village. It seems as though a red and white flame is shooting up from one of the houses."

"You're right," his lieutenant replied.

"It looks as though a fire is beginning to spread," continued the leader. "This whole place will be reduced to ashes in no time. Let's get

out of here."

As quickly as they came, they were gone. The villagers peeked out from their hiding places. All they saw was a hot cloud of dust rising after the galloping horses, but, looking at the village, they saw no fire!

I don't have to describe to you the rejoicing of every member of this fortunate community. Even the little children felt the "Hand of Hashem" on that day. They had all witnessed a great miracle from their Father in Heaven. Little did they know, however, who the true hero was.

That night Reb Yosef had a strange dream. A wonderful feeling overtook him and he felt as though he was being taken into the heavens above. Below him there seemed to be something very familiar. Carefully he looked down again. In house after house were people that he recognized. Yes, it was his very own village. But, wait — one house appeared to be enveloped in fire. Reb Yosef looked again — it was Shimon at his *Gemara* surrounded by flames of holiness.

Reb Yosef awoke the next morning with a great feeling of pride. Now he understood it all. Yes, Hashem had miraculously saved his village but only because of a true Torah scholar by the name of Shimon. The dream was a message from Heaven that the miracle that frightened away the blood-thirsty army was brought about by the young student who wouldn't let fear keep him from his Torah study.

Shimon and his father were surprised that day when a messenger knocked on their door asking them both to come to Reb Yosef's study. No one else was ever told why the village had been saved because Reb Yosef wanted Shimon to remain the same humble boy that he always had been. The old rabbi told Shimon that it was his duty to continue studying Torah because he would surely become a great leader of Israel. Just as the flame of his Torah had frightened away the Cossacks, so it would light the way for the Jewish people.

How The War Was Won

by Rabbi Paysach Krohn

"**H**ey, Label," shouted Avi, "let's go and have a catch. I've got to practice my pitching."

"In half a flash," answered Label. "It's time I learned to make that throw from third base."

The two boys slipped out of their bunk, ran behind their cabin and began playing.

Meanwhile in the next room Simcha was having his daily argument with Chaim. "How about a game of chess, Chaim?"

"Look," said Chaim, with more than a touch of disgust, "you beat me every time we play: I admit you're the greatest, all right? I've never seen anyone like you — all you care about is chess, chess, chess."

"And you," shot back Simcha, "all you care for is stamps, stamps, stamps! Look at that," he continued. "Rest period started only two minutes ago, and your stamp album is already open."

And so it went, everybody taking advantage of "rest period" in Camp Achvah to perfect his own favorite pastime — Avi his pitching, Simcha his chess, Josh his hitting, and Bernie his pillow fights. (Bernie averaged one exploded pillow and two "no night activities" every week due to his feathery exploits.)

But where was Zvi? Well, to find Zvi one would have to look in the camp's *shul*, for there Zvi Brenner studied *dinim* (laws) as ambitiously as the other boys played baseball. Zvi vividly remembered the story his *rebbi,* Rabbi Katz, had told him right before he left for camp. Someone had once asked a renowned rabbi how he had become such a *lamdan* (Torah scholar).

"It only took five minutes," was the reply.

"Five minutes?" blurted out Zvi. "A *talmid chacham* in just five minutes?"

"Yes, five minutes here and five minutes there," explained his *rebbi* — which, of course, meant that even his spare time was spent in learning.

That story made a deep impression on Zvi. He enjoyed pitching, chess, and reading, and he played as hard as anyone else during activities, but his ambition was to become a *talmid chacham,* and he decided to undertake an extra learning period at camp. Thus, during the daily rest period Zvi would go to the *shul* and study *dinim* (Torah law) from his *Shulchan Aruch.* Sometimes he studied with an older counselor, sometimes by himself, but never did he fail to use this free time for learning.

❀ ❀ ❀

The summer rolled on and the boys were enjoying themselves as never before. Avi became pitcher of the camp's Junior Team, and Simcha found a counselor who played chess with him once every day and twice on Fridays. Josh began hitting like never before, and Zvi enjoyed a new outlook on all his actions. No longer did he do *mitzvos* merely out of habit, but rather because he was aware of their meaning, their reason, and exactly how they should be done.

"How good it is to know that you're doing everything the way our great rabbis taught," he thought to himself. "And it takes only a daily rest period to learn so much!" He was sure that Rabbi Katz would be proud of his accomplishment, and that made him feel even better.

❀ ❀ ❀

Finally there were only three weeks left to camp. Now, no matter what any counselor said, every camper knew that without doubt Color

War was around the corner. Let's face it, what is camp without Color War?

Cheers and chants of "1-2-3-4 — We-want-Color-War!" began to rock the dining hall at every meal. Every camper participated, and with each meal their voices grew louder.

One lunchtime, the head counselor rose from his seat and announced: "Sorry boys — you're shouting for nothing. Color War is a waste of time and energy. There just won't be any Color War this year and I'd appreciate it if you'd all stop this nonsensical cheering."

At first the campers were stunned, but then, at the instigation of the oldest bunk, they began again: "1-2-3-4 — We-want-Color-War! 5-6-7-8 — We-don't-want-to-wait!"

Tension mounted — boys raced each other in swimming, played furiously with each other in handball, and ran against each other in relays, all preparing for the big spectacle, the one that separated the men from the boys — the Color War that the head counselor promised would never be.

On the following day, an announcement was made on the P.A. system that a local congressman was coming to camp and that everyone was to get dressed in his *Shabbos* best to greet him.

Within fifteen minutes all campers were assembled and were marching out towards the camp gate when two cars came racing through the gate and stopped suddenly. Five huge men jumped out of each car, with rifles in their hands. The sight was shocking. Some of the youngest boys began crying, while the rest just stood there terrified, hoping that the congressman and his police escort would come soon.

"What do you want?" asked the head counselor, who was leading the "welcoming" party.

"We want your money and your valuables," said one of the men, "and we're desperate — so make it fast!"

"Look here," said the head counselor, "we won't take this from you — if you want our money you'll have to fight for it."

The campers all stood there open-mouthed.

"If that's the way you want it," yelled back one of the hoodlums angrily, "then we'll have war!"

"What kind of war?" snapped the head counselor sharply.

In reply, all ten men pointed their guns towards the sky and unloaded a powerful shot that rocked the camp, and yelled: "Color war!"

The boys were too stunned to believe it, but after a moment's silence they came to their senses and bedlam broke loose. "1-2-3-4 — We-have-Color-War! 5-6-7-8 — No-one-has-to-wait!"

"Attention, please, all campers go to *minchah,* learning groups, supper. Teams will be announced after supper," blared a sobering voice over the loudspeaker. The pandemonium died down and ordinary excitement prevailed for the rest of the afternoon.

The boys could not relax or even eat, for they still could not rest.

Supper seemed to take a year, but finally the teams were announced. The head counselor also announced that new things had been added to this year's Color War competitions. The generals would inform their teams about it.

The boys soon found out that, among other thrilling additions, there was a brand new *Halachah* (Torah Law) contest. Boys knowing *dinim* would earn points for their team — points that could eventually spell the difference between victory and defeat. Not too many boys knew of Zvi's learning, so everyone thought his team had an equal chance to win. That night before going to bed and the next morning before line-up, the boys began studying the *Shulchan Aruch* earnestly.

The war was on. The teams were named *Chessed* and *Mishpat* — Kindness vs. Judgment, Charity vs. Law. Zvi was assigned to the *Chessed* team, and at the start of the first day, *Chessed* took a quick lead, winning most of the sports. The *Halachah* contest was to be on the last day, to give everyone ample time to learn and memorize as much as possible.

Songs, cheers, skits, and plays — this Color War was a real thriller. At the end of the first complete day, *Chessed* still led but by very little — three points. It seems that *Mishpat* had caught up because of more original songs and snappier marches.

More competition — grand marches, theme banners, bunk decorations, inspirational speeches — everyone was on the go, and in every spare moment learning a *halachah*. The skits were funny, the banners were beautiful — everyone was working hard.

After a day and a half, *Mishpat* led 375 to 371, and they seemed to be gaining. The boys were then told that the score would no longer be announced until the final count was in.

It was close and everyone knew it. Zvi realized that he knew many *dinim,* but he did not want to show how much he knew. He did not want others to consider him a *talmid chacham,* or a show-off. He had only tried to follow his *rebbi's* advice, and in the bargain he had learned many *halachos* this summer.

He continued to debate in his mind — should he enter the contest or should he not? What about his team? Everyone was doing his best. Was he doing his best by disqualifying himself? Another point seemed to bother him — Rabbi Katz had told him that the ideal way to learn was *lishmah* — for the sake of study itself, and not to get payment or points.

Zvi finally decided to go to Rabbi Eisenberg, the rabbi of the camp, with his problem. Rabbi Eisenberg welcomed Zvi to his room and asked him to sit down, and listened quietly to Zvi's problem. After some thought the Rabbi told him to enter the contest and to answer all the questions he was asked. "Not only some, but *all*," he emphasized. "Of course camp is a place for sports, exercise, and fresh air, but the *mitzvah* to study Torah never takes a vacation. Who knows? Other boys may admire what you accomplished this summer and they may be inspired to imitate you. Thanks to you, more Torah will be studied."

Rabbi Eisenberg put his hand on Zvi's head for a moment and Zvi's insides almost melted with happiness.

True, Avi pitched a beautiful game for *Mishpat* that morning, and the victory put them 15 points ahead; Bernie swam across the pool leaving the others lengths behind, to further fatten the *Mishpat* lead; but no one even came close to Zvi's masterful answers in the *halachah* quiz. The judges marveled and all the spectators stared in disbelief as the youngster of eleven recited *din* after *din*. After Zvi's recitation new hope sprang up in the hearts of the *Chessed* team, and the *Mishpat* members suspected that they had met their end.

The Grand Sing was all one-sided, as even the counselors of the *Mishphat* team could not persuade their boys that they had a chance. They sang with no fervor whatsoever, while *Chessed* sang like never before.

When the score was announced that night, the *Chessed* team was delirious, and unrestrained joy broke loose in the *Chessed* half of the recreation hall. Everyone then knew Zvi Brenner had taken the *Chessed* team from the depths of defeat and single-handedly led them to victory in Color War. The boys jumped, danced, and cheered as the team's general and Zvi were lifted high in the air. Yes, Zvi certainly had done a *Chessed* to his team mates — and passed *Mishpat* on his opponents!

The Lost Page

by Rabbi Moshe Yechiel Friedman

His name was Sholom. He was just ten years old. His family lived in a small town where there was no day school and, although his parents were making arrangements to move to a larger Jewish community, they didn't want Sholom's Torah education to suffer meanwhile. So they sent him to live with his grandparents where he could go to a yeshivah until the family could be together again. Sholom lived with his grandfather and grandmother in the big, yellow house on Weaver Road.

Strange that his name should be Sholom, he often thought. Sholom means peace, and he did not feel at peace. In the home of his grandparents he was very unhappy. Grandfather and Grandmother loved him dearly, and he returned their love. But, there were things about his grandparents that bothered Sholom, especially since he loved them so much.

Sholom's grandfather was a pious and learned man. He owned a small business that kept him busy most of the day. At home, he spent his time either bending over a *sefer* or helping unfortunate people. He had hopes that some day Sholom would become a big *talmid chacham* (Torah scholar) and a source of true Jewish pride. So Sholom was sent to a yeshivah where he would be taught the things that every Jewish child should know, but Sholom was not completely happy with Grandfather's plans for his future.

To Sholom, Grandfather's world didn't have enough excitement or adventure, fame or fortune. The old man's routine seemed very dull to a little boy like Sholom who had gone to public school for most of his life. Sholom did not see what Grandfather gained from his constant study. Even the people living on Weaver Road hardly knew Grandfather, much less strangers from the great wide world. So it was that Grandfather's thoughts about Sholom's future and Sholom's *own* thoughts were quite different. No wonder Sholom was a very unhappy child.

One sunny afternoon, Sholom sat before an open *Gemara* with his eyes looking up at the bright blue sky outside. Grandfather had asked him to review the *Gemara* he had learned in class that day. Sholom was doing poorly in school, and his teacher said he had to study more at home. But Sholom could not concentrate on the printed page. His mind was full of thoughts very far removed from the contents of the day's lesson. He sat absorbed in his thoughts, his back reclining against the chair, his two arms laid out straight on the pages of his open *Gemara*.

The window was open, and a gust of wind carried a cinder into his left eye. The sudden sting caused Sholom to raise his arm quickly, not realizing that the page of the *Gemara* had become stuck to his sweaty arm! When he lifted his hand, the page of the *Gemara* ripped, from the top of the page down to the very bottom. The torn leaf fluttered down towards the floor, but suddenly it was caught up by another gust of wind that blew in through the window. Almost before Sholom realized what had happened, the page was carried out of the window and disappeared from sight.

For a moment, Sholom was stunned. The page was gone! Now he could not possibly study, even if he wanted to. What concerned him even more was that Grandfather might think that he had torn out the page on purpose, to free himself from his study. Sholom knew that he had never been dishonest, but did Grandfather know that? The thought that Grandfather might distrust him, even a little, hurt Sholom so much that it brought tears to his eyes.

While these thoughts were flashing through his mind, Sholom was out of his chair and racing for the door. He opened the door and stepped into the street. For a moment, he was dazzled by the bright sunlight that shone outdoors. Then he looked up and down the street to see if he could find the fugitive page. It was nowhere in sight. Sholom began walking slowly down the street, making a careful inspection every step of the way. Perhaps in this way he might recover the missing page.

Every now and then, there was a fresh gust of wind. When that happened, Sholom looked up, hoping the wind would lift the page into the air once again. After carrying on his search for half a block, the first sign of hope appeared. A strong breeze swept down the street, and Sholom noticed what seemed to be the missing page floating in the air. It flew into the open window of a large brick house, twenty yards from him. Sholom's heart beat rapidly as he hurried down the street and came to a halt in front of the house.

Not until he had pushed the buzzer outside the door did Sholom realize who the owner of the house was. He and his friends had often passed here with a feeling of awe and deep admiration. This was the home of Captain Steve Green, a pilot for Trans-Atlantic Airlines. Every once in a while, Capt. Green would be seen on Weaver Road dressed in his snappy pilot's uniform and would be admired by everyone. No wonder Sholom's heart skipped a few beats when he heard the sound of footsteps approaching behind the door. The knob turned and the door opened, revealing the broad-shouldered figure of the flier dressed in brown slacks and tan sport shirt. The vision at such close range of Weaver Road's hero left Sholom speechless.

"Well, young man," Steve Green asked the awestruck Sholom, "what can I do for you?"

Slowly the power of speech returned to Sholom. "Well, you see," Sholom began, still very nervous, "it's like this. I'm looking for a page, a printed page, with special words ... "

"Look here, boy," Green interrupted, "Why don't you just come inside and tell me all about it there. No sense in standing out here when we could just as well be inside."

Sholom followed the big figure of the pilot into the house. The house was tastefully furnished and kept in fine condition. Against one wall was a glass-walled case containing a number of trophies that Steve Green had won during his flying career. Sholom could not have been more impressed had he walked into the office of the President of the United States. Following his host, he found himself in the living room. Steve motioned to one of the chairs, and Sholom sat down.

"Now let's start from the beginning," the flier said. "What seems to be bothering you?"

Seated in the soft, comfortable chair, Sholom began to compose himself. His mission was simple enough, yet he did not quite know how to begin. The whole thing seemed a little silly, come to think of it. What right did he have to come into a stranger's house in search of a lost piece of paper? But it was too late now. Sholom had to explain.

"Well, you see it's this way, Capt. Green," Sholom began. "I don't go to the same kind of school that most other boys go to. I go to a special school that's called a yeshivah. Did you ever hear of a yeshivah, sir?"

Steve Green nodded. For a moment his eyes seemed to gaze into the distance as though he had forgotten where he was. Quickly he aroused himself from his daydream and spoke.

"Yes, I've heard of a yeshivah."

"Well," Sholom continued, "in this yeshivah we learn special subjects. One of them is called *Gemara*. Did you every hear of *Gemara*, Capt. Green?"

"Yes, I've heard of *Gemara*."

"You did!" Sholom exclaimed, "well, that's really something. Anyway, here's what happened. I was sitting in my house next to the window and a page tore out of my *Gemara* and flew into the street. I think maybe I saw it fly into the window of your house on the second floor. I'm sorry to disturb you, but I need that page very much. You see, that's just the page that I'm supposed to study ... and it's not going too well."

"Well," Green said, "let's go upstairs and see if you're right."

As Sholom followed Green up the stairs one thought kept running through his head over and over again. How did Steve Green know what *Gemara* was? No matter how he tried to push this question out of his mind, it kept coming back over and over. Finally, when they reached the second floor landing, Sholom could no longer restrain his curiosity.

"Capt. Green," Sholom said sheepishly, "may I ask you a question?

It may sound silly, but I would like to know something."

"Why of course," Green replied, "go right ahead. You don't have to be ashamed."

"Well," Sholom began hesitantly, "could you please tell me — if you don't mind — how come you know about *Gemara?*"

"Why shouldn't I?" Steve Green asked, his eyes laughing as he spoke.

"Well, you're a pilot, aren't you? And I never heard of a pilot studying *Gemara*. Do they really teach pilots *Gemara*? Does *Gemara* help you fly a plane?"

"Well, not exactly," replied the pilot, laughing good-naturedly. "The fact is that I didn't learn about *Gemara* while I was in flying school. A long, long time ago when I was a little boy, I also went to a school that was something like a yeshivah. It was called a *cheder*. That's where I learned what *Gemara* is about."

"You mean that you once went to something like a *yeshivah!*" Sholom cried out in amazement. "Well, that's really something."

"Why?" Steve Green inquired. "What's so strange about that?"

"Well, nothing," Sholom stammered out a reply, "except that flying is such a wonderful kind of life, full of excitement and adventure, while learning *Gemara* is so — well, it's not very exciting or interesting. So that's why I didn't think that somebody who was a pilot would know anything about *Gemara*."

Steve Green paused a moment thoughtfully before he spoke again to Sholom. He spoke slowly and his voice seemed to shake a little. "You know, son, I think there's something that I ought to tell you, something that I hope you'll remember for a long time to come. If you do, it will do you quite a bit of good."

Sholom leaned forward intently to hear every word that his hero said. Steve Green was talking to him from the very bottom of his heart.

"When I was as old as you are," Steve continued, "I thought the way you think now. To me, the *cheder* seemed a very dull place, and the *rebbi* a very unimportant person. I wanted excitement and adventure, and I chose a pilot's career to find it. And right now after being a pilot for many years, I can tell you that things look a lot different now than they did when I was a boy."

"Are you sorry you became a pilot?" Sholom asked, not able to believe his ears.

"Maybe I shouldn't say I'm sorry," Steve reflected aloud, "but I will say that there was a lot more in that piece of *Gemara* than I realized. After flying for so many years, it's like any other job. There isn't very much excitement left. But I know that whatever little *Gemara* I learned as a boy becomes more exciting and more full of meaning as the years go by. And I'm sure that you'll feel the same way, if you study real hard."

Sholom stood as if he was hypnotized. Capt. Steve Green's words had reached deep down into his soul and left a mark that could never be erased. How well he understood his grandfather now, and how beautiful his way of living appeared to Sholom now. He stood immersed in his thoughts until Steve Green's voice fell upon his ears once more.

"There it is," the pilot said, "the page you're looking for is on the floor by the window." Green picked up the page and stared at it sadly. He said, "Yes, my boy, I really wish I had spent more time studying *Gemara*. But you had better get back home. Your folks might be worrying about you."

Sholom took the lost page. He held it tenderly, kissed it and clasped it to his bosom. He knew that he would study this page until he was as familiar with it as he was with the house where he lived. He held out his hand to Steve Green and said goodbye. He was too choked up inside to say anything more. The hero of Weaver Road grasped Sholom's hand firmly and walked him downstairs to the front door. He watched Sholom walk down the street and waved when Sholom turned around for one last glimpse. Then Sholom walked straight to his grandfather's house, his head held high and the lost page pressed tightly against his breast.

The Unexpected Prize

by Rabbi Moshe Yechiel Friedman

You see, Danny Ehrens was a dreamer.

Now Danny didn't dream all the time. Sometimes he would listen intently as his rebbi carefully explained a sentence of the *Chumash* or a line of *Rashi*. And when the rebbi told a story or spoke about the holidays and their meaning, Danny never failed to gulp down every word hungrily. During such moments, Danny used to bite squarely on the middle of his thumbnail. This helped him chase away the uninvited thoughts that used to come into his head. Most of the time, though, Danny just dreamed — especially on a sunny day.

A bright sunbeam would fall upon the *Chumash,* or a robin's warbling note would come through the open window, and Danny's head would turn to the wide blue sky outside like a sunflower following the sun. Just for a minute, Danny told himself. He was sure that he was going to look right back into the *Chumash* again in a moment. But once his eyes left the little black words on the page and turned towards the heavens, strange things happened to Danny.

As he looked up into the blue above, the sounds of the classroom grew fainter and fainter. The voices of the boys reciting the day's lesson were barely audible, and even the *rebbi's* deep voice barely reached his ears. In these dreamy flights of fancy, Danny traveled to distant times and distant places. He was living thousands of miles away. And in all these dreams, whenever they came, Danny was always a hero.

But Danny wasn't just any kind of hero. He always imagined himself to be the sort of hero that he used to hear about when the *rebbi* told stories to the class. Sometimes he was King David. Danny could just see himself, sling in hand, stepping out from the ranks of Israel's army to face the mighty giant, Goliath. Fearlessly, he aimed his sling and struck the huge warrior a fatal blow. Then he cut off the fallen warrior's head and returned to the Jewish camp in triumph and glory.

And sometimes he was Moshe. With his staff in hand, Danny came before the powerful Pharaoh and demanded that he set the Jews free. Then he would be standing at the Sea of Reeds, ordering his fellow Jews to march forward, or he would be standing before a huge rock, striking it with his staff and causing a river of water to gush out to the thirsty Jewish nation.

Most of all, though, Danny liked to be Avraham, destroying the idols of his father, Terach, over and over again. And how steadfast he was when he refused Nimrod's demand to deny his faith in the only G−d! Without even a flutter of his heart, he allowed himself to be thrown into the blazing furnace. Then the great miracle took place, and Danny saw himself strolling about unharmed amid the raging flames.

Only in his dreams, however, was Danny a hero. In real life, he was far from the dashing figure of his reveries. He really wasn't exceptional in anything. When the boys played baseball, Danny was sent far out into the outfield where he spent almost all of his time watching bees or chasing butterflies. If he went on a hike with his friends, he was always ten or fifteen yards behind the others. In his studies, too, Danny lagged behind the other boys. No matter how hard he tried, he never could manage to keep up. A few years back, somebody once told Danny that he had a head like a block of wood, and by now Danny was ready to agree.

You have no idea how much Danny wanted to be a good student. He studied by himself. He studied with his friends. He studied with his father. But it just didn't seem to do any good. It was just as though his mind was locked up in a vault and nobody knew the combination. Time after time, whenever a marking period ended, Danny hoped that perhaps this time his report card would show improvement. Time after time, Danny was disappointed. It hurt him terribly that his friends were so much better in their studies, but what could he do? He would have given almost anything to be able to show his marks proudly as the bright pupils in the class always did, but it seemed that he never would.

There's one thing, though, that everyone could tell you. Maybe Danny didn't have a good head, but he certainly had a good heart. He would do anything for anybody. The whole neighborhood knew that Danny used to deliver groceries every morning for old Mrs. Kempler, who was too feeble to walk down from the second floor. On Fridays, Danny would make two trips to make sure the woman had everything she needed for *Shabbos*. This was just one of Danny's many fine deeds. Among Danny's friends, not one could remember ever asking him a favor and being refused. It's no wonder that Danny was liked by everybody, even though he wasn't exactly a shining star when it came to some other things.

Danny was naturally good-hearted, but that wasn't the only reason he acted that way. The main reason Danny did these kind deeds because he was trying to be like his favorite hero, Avraham. Danny had listened with wonder when his *rebbi* told how Avraham had prepared a sumptuous feast for the three angels who came to visit, thinking that they were weary travelers. He had been even more impressed by Avraham's prayers for the people of Sidom, who were so terribly wicked. What a kind person Avraham must have been to plead with Hashem even for a city that had committed so many sins. Stories like these made Danny decide that he, too, would try to be like Avraham and try to help as many people as he could.

Sometimes, in fact, Danny was a little too anxious to help a needy person. On his way to class one day, Danny was stopped by a man with a puzzled look on his face. From the way he dressed and spoke, Danny guessed that this man came from a different part of the country.

"Excuse me, son," the stranger said to Danny, "could you tell me where I can find Ivory Street?"

Danny's heart leaped with joy. Here was a chance to help somebody who really was in need of assistance. "Oh, sure," Danny replied excitedly, "it's not far from here. All you have to do is walk three blocks down Grant Street, cross over at Abner's delicatessen, walk half a block to Sheldon, turn left, walk another two blocks, turn right a little bit, and after you pass the stationery story, there you are."

Danny was so busy giving directions that he didn't notice the change that came over the man's face. Now that Danny was finished, he looked up at him. The man looked much more confused now than he had before Danny offered directions. Evidently, the visitor hadn't any idea how to proceed to Ivory Street. There seemed to be only one other solution to the problem.

The man had stopped Danny near Galt's barber shop. Danny glanced through the store window at the large electric clock hanging from the wall. He had only fifteen minutes until class. Quickly, he made calculations. Let's see now. To Grant would take about four minutes, half a minute to Sheldon, and maybe if we walked very fast — and maybe just this once my *rebbi* might come a few minutes late … "You know what, Mister," Danny finally concluded out loud, "I'll walk over there with you."

Quickly the man answered, "Oh, no, I don't want to take you out of your way. I'll manage to get there. Thanks a lot."

But Danny would not accept a refusal. Making an about face, he headed towards Grant Street. The stranger had no choice but to follow him. Danny covered the three blocks in record time, half walking and half trotting. Every block or so he would stop to wait until his follower, puffing and out of breath, caught up with him. At Abner's Delicatessen, Danny crossed as soon as the light changed, noticing at the same time that the bank clock on the other side of the street now read five minutes to the hour. The rest of the distance to Ivory Street was practically a race between Danny, who hadn't come to class late even once this term, and the gasping stranger, who plodded along as quickly as he could, so as not to lose sight of his young guide. Finally, the two figures reached a crowded corner, and Danny, too breathless to speak, happily pointed to a street sign that read "Ivory Street."

The man let out a deep breath of relief. "Well, son," he said to Danny gratefully, "we finally made it. I guess," he continued as he put his hand into his pocket, "I owe you a little something for your trouble." He pulled out a coin and offered it to Danny.

Danny was shocked. "Oh, no," he exclaimed. "I can't take money for a *mitzvah*. I was just happy to do you a favor. But I have to hurry now, or else I'll be late to class."

"Well, thanks a lot, son. I really appreciate —" But before he could complete his sentence, Danny was already streaking like a well-aimed arrow back to his class in the hope that by some miracle he might get there in time.

When Danny finally reached the door of his classroom, his heart fluttered nervously. All was quiet inside except for the voice of Rabbi Plesnick, who was teaching a new portion of the *Chumash*. Danny's face was crimson with embarrassment as he gently turned the doorknob. Bit by bit he opened the door, hoping to make as little disturbance as possible. Luckily, Rabbi Plesnick was so absorbed in explaining a difficult sentence that he did not notice the silent figure tiptoeing along the side of the room, across the back, and toward the seat right next to the window on the far side of the room. Danny rejoiced. He had made the trip to his seat without disrupting the class.

Gradually, Danny began to crouch down so that he could place himself into his chair. As he did so, his eyes happened to wander towards the *rebbi's* desk. There, to Danny's amazement, was something that hypnotized him — and did not let him move an inch further. Right next to Rabbi Plesnick's motioning hand, standing side by side in an even row, was the most beautiful set of *Chumashim* Danny had ever seen. The covers were a rich-looking maroon and gleaming gold, and the edges of the pages were also painted gold. To Danny, these volumes were like five brave horsemen marching together into the sunlight. Never in his life had Danny ever wished for anything as he now wished to be the proud owner of these precious *Chumashim*.

But what were these *seforim* (books) doing on Rabbi Plesnick's desk? Slowly, Danny came out of his trance and settled into his seat. Maybe the other boys knew. Danny felt that he just couldn't stand the suspense of waiting until the class came to an end. He tried to look into his own *Chumash* and forget about the glittering treasure in front of the room, but every few minutes, of their own accord, his eyes would leap up for just one last glimpse. The more Danny saw the proud

volumes, the more convinced he became
that someday he must become the owner of a set exactly like that one. And not
only that. Danny was perfectly sure that
if he could study from such a magnificent set of *Chumashim*, he would
become a wonderful student, and before
long he would be
the pride of Rabbi
Plesnick's class.

How he had
managed to sit still
until the class ended,
Danny never knew. As
soon as Rabbi Plesnick
gave the signal for dismissal,
Danny hurried over to Gaby Hill-
man and caught him just as he was
going out the door.

"Hey, Gaby," Danny asked eagerly,
"what are those *Chumashim* on Rabbi Plesnick's desk? Aren't they
beautiful?"

Gaby looked at Danny quizzically. "Didn't you hear what he said
this morning right after class began?" he asked.

"No, I didn't," Danny replied. "You see, I got in a little late. I must
have come in after Rabbi Plesnick had finished talking about it."

"Oh, well, I might as well tell you, although it probably won't
make much of a difference. Everybody knows that Mord Hollis will win
the prize anyway."

By now Danny's curiosity was bubbling over. "Come on, Gaby,"
he pleaded, "I still don't know what it's all about. What kind of a
prize?"

"Well, you see, it's this way. This morning Rabbi Plesnick came in with this set of *Chumashim* and he told the class that he's going to run some kind of a contest. Whoever wins the contest gets the *Chumashim* as a prize, but what's the difference. You won't win it, and neither will I. It's a sure thing for Mord Hollis."

"Oh, come on," Danny insisted, "tell me what kind of a contest."

"It's a contest on all of *Sefer Bereishis,*" Gaby answered impatiently. "There'll be about fifty questions on all the *sidras* that we learned. But it's not just on the *Chumash* alone. Rabbi Plesnick expects us to find out everything that *Rashi* says, and the *Midrash* and *Gemara,* too."

"But how are we supposed to know these things?"

"We asked the same thing. Rabbi Plesnick said that if we want to win the prize badly enough we could ask our fathers or other people to help us out. He told us: '*Ein davar omeid bifnei haratzon* — nothing can stop you if you really want something. And he said...' "

As Gaby continued to explain, Danny's eyes began to have that dreamy, far-away look that he used to get when he glanced out of the classroom window up into the blue sky. My, just imagine Danny winning that prize! Already he could see how the *Chumashim* would look on his dresser — right next to his framed portrait of the *Chofetz Chaim.* He imagined himself lovingly opening the glittering covers and handling the pages with an ever-so-gentle touch. He saw himself bending over the sacred words, studying diligently for hours on end. Danny was suddenly brought back to reality by Gaby's last statement.

"But as I say," Gaby said as he turned to go, "Mord Hollis is sure to win."

Mordechai Hollis. All the boys called him Mord. Everybody knew that Mord was the brightest boy in the class. And Mord knew it, too. If he heard something once, Mord could remember it forever. He understood whatever the *rebbi* said even before the words were out of his mouth. Just for fun, Mord would sometimes play a question game with some of the other boys in the class. They would ask each other questions about the *Chumash* and see who knew best. Mord would always win. There was no doubt that all the boys would study hard for Rabbi Plesnick's contest, but everybody agreed that Mord would win the prize.

Did Danny have any chance at all to be the winner of the contest? As he walked out the door and through the hallway, Danny became more and more convinced that he had. True enough, Mord Hollis was much smarter than he was and remembered things that Danny forgot a long, long time ago. But what was it that Rabbi Plesnick had said? — "*Ein davar omeid bifnei haratzon.*" Try hard enough, and you're bound to succeed. Well, Danny was willing to try as hard as he knew how, and that way he just *had* to succeed.

That very same night, a tremendous change came over Danny. Someone would think he had been hypnotized. Even before he sat down to supper, Danny opened his *Chumash Bereishis* and began to swallow up the black lines with his eyes. When he sat down to the table, the open *Chumash* was before him, propped up on the plastic napkin holder. Danny hardly knew what food his mother set before him. Even his favorite dessert could not take his mind off his studying. Only one thought kept on going through Danny's mind. He must win those *Chumashim* … he must win them … he must!

Danny's father and mother were very upset over his actions. Of course, they were anxious for him to become a good student and they would have been proud if he came home with both arms embracing a beautiful set of *Chumashim*. At the same time, they were worried that too much study might not be good for Danny's health. The contest was only two weeks off, however, so they decided not to discourage him too strongly.

During these two weeks, Danny spoke to many people that he never even dreamed of meeting. He went over to the rabbi of the *shul* and asked him to tell him all about *Bereishis*. He visited Mr. Berzin who was known to be a big *talmid chacham* (Torah scholar) and listened hungrily to the *Midrashim* and other stories that dealt with *Bereishis*. He took the biggest *Chumash* that he could find and made his father tell him all the explanations that were found inside. And strangely enough, Danny remembered all the things that he heard. Gone was his old trouble of forgetfulness. Without even realizing it, Danny's memory had undergone a wonderful change. His head was like a steel trap, and nothing that entered could ever escape. Day by day, Danny became more and more confident that he could win the prize. Of course, Mord Hollis would also be studying very hard during these weeks, but Danny felt that this was one time that Mord was in for a real surprise.

As the day of the contest drew near, the boys began to sense that a change had come over Danny. They had formed small groups to ask each other questions in preparation for the contest. Sometimes questions came up that no one in the group could answer. Then one of them would go around to the others looking for an answer. At first, nobody ever asked Danny any of these difficult questions. Who would expect Danny to know the answer if they weren't able to find it among themselves? Once in a while, though, Danny overheard one of these questions, and without even hesitating he would produce the answer immediately. At first the boys were amazed that Danny should know these things, but after a while they took it for granted. More and more you would hear somebody say, "Let's ask Danny. He ought to know." And Danny did know — almost every time. The boys began to treat their classmate with admiration, and Danny drove himself even harder so that his friends would not be disappointed in him. When the day of the contest arrived, every student knew that Danny Ehrens had a very,

very good chance of winning the *Sefer Bereishis* contest — that is, every student except one.

The one exception was Mord Hollis. It never occurred to Mord that anyone else in the class would have a chance to win the treasured prize. Of course, he knew that the other boys would be trying hard, but what chance did they have against him? In fifteen minutes Mord could learn more than the other boys could in a full hour. And Mord made sure that he spent a good number of hours daily absorbing everything he could about *Sefer Bereishis.* Why then, he thought, should he have anything to worry about? Since Mord didn't feel it necessary to join any of the study groups, he didn't even realize that the Danny he saw a few days before the contest was not at all like the Danny he knew on the day that Rabbi Plesnick first brought the set of *Chumashim* to class. As far as Mord Hollis was concerned, the *Chumashim* were as good as his already. In fact, he even felt a little bad that all the other boys had worked so hard in vain.

The great day finally arrived. As the boys filed into the classroom, you could feel the tension and the excitement in their hearts. By some strange accident, Mord and Danny were the last ones to enter the room. Only then did Mord notice that some kind of change had taken place in Danny. Danny's eyes were keen and expectant now, not dull and cloudy as they always had been in the past. He walked with his head higher and his back straighter. Somehow, without knowing just why, Mord suddenly felt a little unsure of himself. Quickly he shrugged his shoulders and walked to his seat.

As Danny entered the room behind Mord, all eyes turned towards him. Danny felt like a boxer about to enter the ring before a championship fight. His heart beat rapidly and his forehead felt a little damp. His throat felt tight and dry. Not looking at the faces that turned towards him as he passed by, he hurried towards his seat near the window. All eyes were now turned towards the door where Rabbi Plesnick would soon appear to begin the anxiously awaited contest.

A few moments later, the figure of Rabbi Plesnick appeared in the doorway of the classroom. He paused a moment at the threshold, then entered. A package of papers, held together by a broad brown rubber band, lay in the folded palm of his hands. As he approached the desk, the boys smelled the mimeograph ink which was still moist and fresh. Rabbi Plesnick stopped at the front of the room, and, as the class watched every one of his movements with fascination, he placed the papers at the center of his desk. With the eyes of his pupils still upon him, he walked over to the corner closet and removed a package. *It was the set of prize Chumashim.* This too, was placed on his desk.

Rabbi Plesnick greeted the class as usual. Instead of the customary chorus of replies, however, his words were met by silence. The boys were too tense to engage in courtesies on this historic day.

"Well, boys," Rabbi Plesnick coaxed with a smile, "aren't you going to answer me?"

A few embarrassed murmurs emerged from the front seats. A boy in the back giggled nervously.

The rebbi sensed the strain in the classroom.

"Well, boys," he announced thoughtfully, "I suppose I don't have to tell you that this is the day we have all been waiting for. I can see that everyone of you has worked very hard during the past weeks, and you are all anxious to get started. Before we actually get on with the contest, however, I would like to make a few remarks to you. Maybe you will feel a little more relaxed after I am through."

The boys leaned forward to hear what the teacher was about to say.

"The purpose of this contest," Rabbi Plesnick explained, "is not just to see how eager you boys are to win a set of *Chumashim.* That in itself would give you a wrong idea. The reward that a person gets for learning Torah is much greater than anything that I or anybody else can give you. What I felt was that in preparing yourself for a contest like this, you would get some idea how great and vast our Torah really is. You would begin to understand how much meaning there is even in a single word of the *Chumash.* So no matter who wins the contest, you are really all winners because you have all gained something very valuable. This does not mean that you should try less hard to win. But it *does* mean that the chance of not winning should not seem so terrible, nor should it make you feel that all your effort was wasted."

The rebbi waited to see what effect his words would have upon his pupils. He could see that they were deeply impressed. But he also knew that their hearts were still pounding in expectation of the contest.

"All right, boys," he said cheerfully, "let's begin."

A rustle passed through the classroom as the boys adjusted themselves in their seats. The sighs of relief that escaped their lips showed that they were anxious to start. Some of them had already begun to finger their pencils nervously. In the far corner of the room, Danny brushed his sleeve against his face to wipe away the perspiration that was beginning to form on his forehead.

Rabbi Plesnick called one of his students over to his desk. He gave the pack of papers to the boy with instructions on how to pass them out to the class. While the student moved back and forth between the rows of seats, placing a sheet of paper face down on each desk, the rebbi gave additional information about the contest.

"While these papers are being passed out," Rabbi Plesnick said, "let me tell you something about them. There are thirty questions on these papers, all on *Chumash Bereishis.* The first few questions will be easy, but they will become more and more difficult afterwards. The last few questions will be very hard. The answers should be written in the space provided at the end of each question. You will be allowed one full hour to complete them."

The rebbi paused. Several seconds passed, and a pupil raised his hand. Heads turned towards him in curiosity. Rabbi Plesnick nodded in the direction of the lifted hand.

"What happens," the boy asked "if there's a tie?"

The grin that spread like jelly over his face showed that he thought himself very clever to have thought of such a possibility.

"I'm glad someone thought of that," the *rebbi* replied. "At least you're not sleepy-heads. The truth is that this question bothered me quite a bit. But I have a plan that should take care of such a situation. At the end of the thirty questions, there will be one extra question which I myself will ask you. The first one who thinks he has the right answer will come up to my desk and whisper it in my ear. Whoever gets the right answer first, will get credit for that question. In that way, there is little chance of there being a tie. If this doesn't work out, we'll have to think of something else later."

There were no other questions. Now that the contest had been fully explained, Rabbi Plesnick gave the signal to begin. The long awaited moment had arrived.

Quickly the boys began to fumble for their papers and pencils. The first few questions were answered in rapid succession. The eyes of the students moved swiftly back and forth across the page as though they were watching a tennis match. After the tenth question, however, the feverish activity began to slow down. The hurried scratching of pencils against the hard surfaces of the desks gradually subsided. The questions could no longer be answered at a glance. The room became almost silent, and only an occasional noise broke the stillness.

Danny was too engrossed in answering the questions to observe what the rest of the class was doing. When he was just about halfway finished, he sat back a moment to rest. During this brief pause,

Danny was able to make a survey of the class. What he saw left him with a strange mixture of feelings.

First, he was surprised that several boys had already reached the point of surrender. Evidently, they had not been prepared for questions as difficult as the ones that lay before them. One of his friends was staring at the ceiling while his pencil drooped from his mouth at a careless angle. At the far end of the room, another pupil was absent-mindedly chewing the top of his eraser. A third boy was resting his head on his outstretched arm, seeking a minute's relaxation from the day's strain.

These sights made Danny's heart flutter with nervousness. Although he now found it necessary to stop and think before replying to the questions, he still felt confident that he would know all the answers. A sly smile began to steal over Danny's face. He felt guilty about it, but he could not keep himself from being delighted over the fact that he knew the answers better than some of his friends.

As he looked further about the room, Danny's hopes rose still higher. He could see that even the bright students in the class were having difficulty. Most of them were staring intently at their papers, trying to reach into their minds for information. At the halfway mark, Danny seemed to be having an easier time than his classmates. The smile on his face began to spread a little wider.

Suddenly, Danny's smile was interrupted, and his heart took a quick leap. Out of the corner of his eye, he caught a glimpse of Mord Hollis. Mord was bent over his paper, working smoothly and steadily. He didn't seem to be having any trouble at all. Danny's hopes reached their crest, and now they slowly began to sink. Maybe the boys were right after all, Danny began thinking to himself. He probably had no chance at all against Mord Hollis. A lump formed in Danny's throat as his heart brimmed with disappointment.

As Danny's hopes began to fade, his attention was arrested by the glint of light which shone from the teacher's desk. A ray of sunlight had just struck the proud *Chumashim* on the teacher's desk, and the gold letters glittered brightly. As Danny's gaze turned towards the splendid volumes, they seemed to beckon to him and give him new encouragement. With fresh resolve, Danny picked up his pencil and resumed his efforts to answer the remaining questions.

Danny had five questions left to answer when he noticed some activity at the front of the room. Rabbi Plesnick had a piece of chalk in his hand and was writing on the blackboard. In large, clear letters, he spelled out, "FIFTEEN MINUTES LEFT." Danny made a quick calculation. He had to answer five questions in fifteen minutes — three minutes to each question. True, these were the most difficult questions of the contest, but there seemed to be time enough. As these thoughts ran through Danny's head, he looked around once more to observe what the other pupils in the class were doing. What Danny saw made his heart thump so loudly that he was sure everybody in the class was able to hear the rapid beats.

As Danny's eyes scanned the classroom, he realized that, with the exception of Mord Hollis, everyone in the class had stopped working. One by one, as they reached the difficult questions of the contest, the boys had put their pencils down in despair. Each pupil felt that if he had studied *just a bit more,* he would have been able to fill in every answer on the paper. It was just that little extra that was missing and now every one of them realized that this made all the difference.

The eyes of the class were now fixed on Mord Hollis and Danny Ehrens, the two remaining contestants. Even Rabbi Plesnick was plainly interested in the outcome of the competition. Danny had seldom been the center of attention in the classroom, and he felt uncomfortable. Quickly he lowered his eyes so they would not meet any other pair of eyes in the room. He bowed his head now, and through secretly raised eyelids he studied Mord Hollis across the room. Mord was still working like a well-oiled machine, his motions betraying no anxiety. Just as Danny was about to proceed to the next question, Mord gently laid down his pen and turned his paper on the other side. The barest trace of a smile hovered about his lips. Fifteen minutes to go, and Mord

Hollis had already completed his answers to the thirty questions of the contest.

Panic gripped Danny. It had never occurred to him that Mord could finish so speedily. Now he was the only one working in the tense atmosphere of the classroom. Danny could hardly think straight with so many eyes focused directly on him. He studied the questions intently, but deep inside he was feeling the sting of disappointment over trailing so far behind Mord Hollis. After a few moments, however, Danny forgot all about Mord and the other spectators in the classroom as he continued to complete the answers to the contest.

Minutes had ticked by swiftly when Danny realized once again that Rabbi Plesnick was writing on the blackboard. "FIVE MINUTES LEFT," read the message. Danny clenched his teeth. Three questions had taken all of ten minutes, and the two most difficult questions of all still remained to be answered. Five minutes to go. Danny summoned up all his powers of concentration in order to carry him through the last two hurdles. He wrinkled his brow and curled up his legs in order to help himself think. With all the energy of a star football player, he tackled the twenty-ninth question.

The next to the last question proved to be more simple than Danny had hoped. Rabbi Plesnick must have felt that any student who could carry on this far had earned a treat. But the thirtieth question was everything that a final question could be. It demanded not only a knowledge of the entire *Sefer Bereishis,* but also an understanding of the meaning of all the events that took place in that portion of the *Chumash.* Danny reached back into the farthest crevices of his memory in order to recall the information and ideas which were required for this answer. For three of the longest minutes in his life, he pondered and pondered in order to discover the few words that would spell a successful end to the written part of the contest. Suddenly a light flashed in Danny's brain. A few sentences that his father had once explained to him contained exactly the thought that was necessary to answer this last question. With his pencil in hand,

Danny pounced on the test paper and hurriedly scrawled the answer before it could escape from his head. As he completed the last stroke of the very last word, Rabbi Plesnick announced to the class, "Please put all pencils down, the written part of the contest is now over."

The clatter of Danny's pencil as it struck the desk was the only sound that followed the teacher's announcement. The rest of the class sat in deep stillness, waiting for Rabbi Plesnick's tie-breaking question. Of course, no one knew if there really was a tie at all. Yet everyone seemed to know that Mord Hollis and Danny Ehrens were the only ones who answered all the questions. Perhaps they knew it from the look of satisfaction that Mord and Danny had on their faces. The class knew how much Rabbi Plesnick's next question would mean to those two students.

Rabbi Plesnick addressed the class once more: "Well, boys," he began, "I suppose you know what is coming next. Right now, I don't know who has completed the contest and who has not. For all I know, perhaps nobody has answered all the questions. But if there is a tie, I would like the matter to be settled right now if possible, even before I take your papers from you."

Rabbi Plesnick paused a moment. He wanted to be certain that the next part of his statement would be heard by everyone.

"Let me remind you," he continued, "of what I already told you before the contest began. I am going to ask the class a question. The question will probably come as a surprise to all of you. If you had difficulty with the questions until now, you will probably find this question much harder to answer. But if any one of you does know the answer, come up to the desk as soon as you think of it. The first, and only the first, pupil who tells me the right answer will be given credit for this question."

The *rebbi* was silent a moment. His eyes swung in an arc back and forth across the room. He was satisfied that everybody was listening to this critical question. "I would like to know," Rabbi Plesnick asked, pronouncing each word slowly and evenly, "what was the name of the mother of Avraham Avinu?"

A shudder passed through the class. Avraham's mother? Of course, Avraham had a mother — but what was her name? She wasn't mentioned in the *Chumash,* that was a sure thing. Still, if the rebbi wanted to know her name, it must have been written someplace. But where? Was there anybody else in the room besides the rebbi who knew the answer?

Half a minute passed, and no pupil stirred from his seat. Rabbi Plesnick waited patiently. "Think," he encouraged the boys. "I'm sure that some of you must have seen or heard the name. Try to remember."

Danny was thinking. He was thinking so hard that his head was splitting. The teacher was right! Danny had seen the name somewhere. Was it in *Rashi?* No, he didn't think so. Perhaps in a *Midrash?* That was a likely place. It wasn't Basyah — that was Pharaoh's daughter. It wasn't — wait! That was it. Like a great flash of lightning in a dark sky, the name of Avraham's mother suddenly appeared with dazzling brightness in Danny's head. Like a spring uncoiling, Danny leaped out of his seat and hurried down the aisle towards the *rebbi's* desk. As he moved along, all eyes followed after him with awe and curiosity. Would Danny be the one to find the correct answer? Even Rabbi Plesnick was anxious to hear what Danny was about to say.

Danny was a few feet from the desk when he suddenly stopped. Across the room he caught sight of a boy rubbing his eyes with both hands, as though trying to wipe away the tears that came through his lids. It was Mord Hollis! But why was he crying? Then Danny understood. Mord was in tears because he feared that Danny would be the winner of the contest. Mord had always been the star of the class. He was sure that he would be the one to bring home the splendid prize. And now it seemed that Danny Ehrens, always the slowest boy in class, was going to be the winner instead.

Danny's heart filled with pity for Mord Hollis. Although he had always considered Mord to be a rival, all past differences were washed away by Mord's tears. Danny was sure that Mord would come up with the right answer, if he had enough time. Come to think of it, one of the boys had once asked Mord this very same question, and Mord knew the correct name immediately. It was probably excitement and nothing else that kept Mord from knowing the answer now. And didn't Mord really deserve the *Chumashim* more that Danny? Hadn't Mord always been an excellent pupil and a pride to his *rebbi* and parents? It was just during the past few weeks that Danny had accomplished anything worth mentioning. But what about the beautiful *Chumashim?* To Danny, they had meant more than anything else in life. Could he give them up so easily?

As Danny stood in hesitation near the front of the class, the words that Rabbi Plesnick had spoken earlier echoed through his mind. The important thing about the contest was not the winning of the prize. What really counted was how well each pupil realized the vast sea of knowledge that lay even in a single word of the Torah. And this Danny had learned full well. Never again would he dream of being a hero while the class was engaged in study. The greatest act of heroism was in the learning of Torah itself. Danny no longer imagined himself a hero like Avraham or Moshe. They were far, far too great for him to imitate. But he could be a small hero, in his very own classroom. And that's what really counted.

While every pupil in the class stared in amazement, Danny slowly made an about face and silently made his way back to his seat in the back of the room.

A few moments later Danny's guess proved to be correct. Mord Hollis did know the answer to the question, and suddenly he recalled what it was. Mord wiped away the moist tears that still clung to his eyelashes and happily raised his hand. Throughout the classroom heads began turning in Mord's direction.

"Yes, Mordechai," Rabbi Plesnick called, "would you like to say something?"

"Yes," replied Mord with a triumphant note in his voice. "I would like to answer the question."

"Very well, Mordechai, come up here and tell it to me."

Mord walked up to the rebbi's desk and whispered into Rabbi Plesnick's ear. The rebbi listened earnestly, nodded, then smiled. "Yes, Mordechai," he announced, "Your answer is correct. Avraham's mother was Amaslai bas Carnebo."

Mord grinned. With a jaunty air he returned to his seat while the rest of the class stared at him with a mixture of envy and awe. Only Danny Ehrens fixed his eyes elsewhere. Although he had withheld the answer voluntarily, he could not altogether hold back his disappointment. The glory Mord was getting from his classmates really should have been his, and Danny had to turn his head towards the window to hide the injured look on his face.

Rabbi Plesnick now addressed the class. "Of course," he began, "you boys are anxious to know who won the contest. Before I can tell you, I'll have to look through all these papers and see how many right answers each one of you has. So let's get back to our studies. Open your *Chumashim* please, and turn to the work which we learned yesterday."

As the class opened their *seforim* and fingered through the pages, Danny sat perfectly still. His eyes were still turned away from the class. He feared that if he stirred, he would burst into tears at once. Rabbi

Plesnick realized that Danny's *Chumash* was not opened, but he pretended not to notice. Although he did not know the explanation for Danny's strange behavior during the last part of the contest, he was able to guess that somehow Danny had just gone through a bad experience. Danny's classmates also sensed that there was good reason for Danny's inattentiveness.

After dismissal, the boys huddled admiringly around Mord Hollis. There seemed hardly a doubt that Mord would be announced the winner on the next day. Mord, too, was just as confident. He joked noisily with his friends as they trooped out the door of the classroom. Only after every other student was gone did Danny lift himself from his seat. Slowly, he dressed himself and picked up his books. He hardly lifted his feet as he lumbered out of the empty classroom. Rabbi Plesnick watched him, and sadly shook his head.

That night Danny hardly touched his supper. Aside from the usual courtesies, he said nothing to his family. His father and mother understood that Danny was troubled, and they felt that it was best to leave him to himself. Past experience had taught them that eventually Danny would tell them of his own accord just what was on his mind. And so it was. Just about bedtime, Danny came over to his father and mother, who were conversing in the kitchen.

His father said, "What would you like to talk about, Danny?"

Swallowing hard to keep from breaking into tears, Danny told his father and mother everything that happened during the contest. "And I'm not going back to that class anymore," he concluded tearfully, "I never want to go there again."

"But Danny," his father said soothingly, "perhaps you wouldn't have won anyways. You might have made some mistakes on the written questions."

"I didn't, I didn't," Danny wept. "I know I had them all right. I really should have won the contest."

"But you gave up the prize willingly, didn't you?" his father argued gently.

"I know, but even so ..." Danny's voice trailed off sorrowfully.

"Let me tell you something, Danny," his father said to him quietly. "Perhaps you won't win your set of *Chumashim,* but you've already won something far more important. You've learned to sacrifice something which you wanted very badly in order to keep someone else from being hurt. That's a lot more than a whole room full of *seforim.* So you really aren't the loser after all."

Danny listened intently. His father's words struck deep in his heart. "Thanks, Dad," he said. "I feel much better now." His steps much lighter now, Danny made off for bed.

As the boys assembled in class on the next day, they chatted excitedly. The talking stopped abruptly when Rabbi Plesnick entered the room. After greeting the class, the *rebbi* once more removed the prize *Chumashim* from the cabinet. Then he spoke to the class.

"I don't suppose," said the *rebbi,* "that you boys will be very surprised when you hear who is the winner of the contest. I looked over the papers last night, and only two boys had all the answers correct: Mordechai Hollis and Daniel Ehrens. Since Mordechai was the first one to answer the question which I asked at the end of the contest, he is the winner. Mordechai, will you please come up here and take your prize."

Mord stood up, but did not move from his seat. "Rabbi Plesnick," he said, "may I say something."

"Of course, Mordechai," the *rebbi* replied. "What would you like to say?"

"You see, Rabbi Plesnick," Mord began, "I did a lot of thinking last night, and I tried to figure out a few things. For instance, why did Danny go up to answer the last question and then suddenly turn back after he looked at me? I think Danny knew the answer and didn't give it to you only because he felt sorry for me."

"Is that true, Danny?" Rabbi Plesnick asked. Danny nodded.

"So you see, Rabbi Plesnick," Mord continued, "the prize really belongs to Danny. I'm telling you all this because Danny made me

realize how selfish I was in wanting to win the prize just for myself. Danny's the real winner of the contest."

For a moment, the classroom was perfectly still. Nobody expected Mord to act this way. Then the silence was broken by the *rebbi*. "Well, Danny, I think Mordechai is right. I'm pretty sure that the class also feels the same way." The boys nodded vigorously in assent. "Well, what do you have to say?"

Danny, at first stunned by what was happening, now smiled sheepishly. "I really don't know what to say," he stammered. "I never expected anything like this."

"Well, then," Rabbi Plesnick said, "I suppose you ought to come up here and get your prize. It's waiting for you."

As he walked up to the desk, the class clapped and cheered. Before he went back to his own seat, Danny walked over to Mord — whom he would always call his best friend from then on — and shook hands.

Was it real? Danny could never recall how he rose out of his seat and went to the *rebbi's* desk to accept his treasured *Chumashim.* He felt as though he had been lifted out of the classroom into another world where everything was too wonderful to describe. Even after he brought the *Chumashim* home he could not believe that they were truly his. Only after he opened the splendid covers and began to study from the beautifully printed pages did he begin to feel that he was truly the owner. Yet even then he realized that the contest had gained him a great deal more than a set of *Chumashim.* His father was right — the contest had taught him to be humble and unselfish no matter how great the cost. This was truly the unexpected prize.

Kobi's Great Decision

by Yaffa Ganz

"I'm awfully sorry, Mrs. Fishman. I just don't see any other solution. It's silly for Kobi to be forced to sit in class for the next three weeks until summer vacation starts. He's just not interested in learning. The principal agrees that he should leave school early and we hope that he'll start again in a better frame of mind in September."

Mrs. Fishman sighed. "I suppose you are right. I don't know what to do with him. He's really a bright boy, but his talent just doesn't seem to be directed towards books. Well, thank you and I hope we can find a solution to the problem during the summer."

When Kobi (which was short for Yaakov) heard the news that afternoon, he did a triple somersault and let out a yell of pure joy!

"That's great! Now I can go to Bubby and Zaidy's farm three weeks early! I almost feel like sending the principal a thank you letter!" His brown eyes twinkled and his dimples came out in full force.

"I'm glad you're so happy," said his father. "But Kobi, it's not funny. What will become of you? Whoever heard of a boy a year before his *Bar Mitzvah* who won't open a *Gemara* or a *Chumash* unless he is forced to? And even then, you sit and daydream! What kind of a Jew will you be? How will you know how to act during your life if you don't learn any Torah?"

"I'll know, Abba. Don't worry. I'll have a farm like Zaidy. I'll know how to grow crops and raise animals and build, just like Zaidy. I don't have to learn so much Torah for that. And you said yourself that Zaidy is *m'kadesh shem shamayim* (sanctifies *Hashem's* Name) every day of his life by the wonderful way he lives."

"Yes I did. I also said that just watching Zaidy is a lesson in *halachah* (Torah Law). But that's because Zaidy has learned hard and long ever since he was a little boy. He's never stopped. You know … on second thought, maybe going to Zaidy is the best thing that could happen to you."

❀ ❀ ❀

So Kobi left the school in his busy crowded Tel Aviv neighborhood and packed to go north to his grandfather's farm in north-central Israel. The next day, Kobi became a welcome guest at the farm of his grandparents.

When Zaidy heard the reason for Kobi's early vacation from school, he thought quietly for a while and said, "I don't know, Kobi. How can you possibly learn to run a farm if you don't learn Torah? You have to know an awful lot of *Mishnah* and *Gemara* and *dinim* (Torah laws)!"

"What does all that have to do with farming? That's the best part of coming here. All I ever hear at home is how I have to sit and learn so I'll know how to act and what to do, but here I can just be me and do good work at the same time!"

"Hmmm … well, we'll see. Meanwhile, I think what I'll do is give you a little piece of land and a few animals all your own and we'll see what kind of a farmer you make."

"That's just great!" said Kobi. "When do I start?"

"You'll have to take care of the mule. And you can also have the new colt to ride, if you want him. And let's see … I think you can manage the wild pigeons in the trees behind the barn. The townspeople pay a good price for their eggs. And last, you can have an acre of the plum orchard and keep the money you make from selling them."

All night long, Kobi dreamt of pigeons and plums, of colts and mules. With the very first ray of sunshine, he was out of bed and dressed. He was in such a hurry to get started, that he finished *Shacharis* a long time before his Zaidy who, as usual, *davened* very slowly and with *kavanah* (thought).

"I think you'd better spend the rest of the day brushing up on some of the basic *halachos* (laws) you'll need to keep things running properly," said Zaidy after lunch.

"Oh no," said Kobi. "I finished school for the year, remember? Abba sent me to this farm to work, not learn. Anyway, what *halachos* do I need to farm? You already showed me how to do my work."

"Since when do Jews learn only in school?" asked Zaidy, shaking his head. "And without Torah, a Jew doesn't know how to do *anything* right. But have it your own way. You'll find out a few things soon enough."

The second morning, Kobi woke up ravenously hungry. "I could eat a few steaks for breakfast," he thought to himself. As soon as he zoomed through *Shacharis* (beating Zaidy again!), he ran into the kitchen.

"What are you doing here so early?" asked Bubby, a bit surprised.

"I came to eat breakfast. Don't we have breakfast today?"

"Not yet we don't. Did you feed the mule and the colt already?"

"Oh, they can wait a little. I'll take care of them as soon as I finish eating."

"Will you now? I don't know what they do on other farms, but here we do things the Torah's way. The animals get fed first."

"What does the *Torah* have to do with my breakfast and feeding the animals?" asked Kobi, a little annoyed. (Kobi got annoyed at his Bubby only when he was *very* hungry!)

"That's the *halachah*," said Bubby. "You have to feed the animals first."

"I bet you're just making that up to tease me," sulked Kobi.

Bubby got very insulted. "Young man, you have my permission to check up on me. Tonight you will sit down with your Zaidy and learn the *halachah*. And now will you please go out and feed your animals?"

The rest of the day passed by in hard work, but Kobi loved every minute of it. At night, he asked his Zaidy about feeding the animals before he himself ate.

"Of course it's a *halachah*. come here, I'll show you." He went to his big bookcase and took out a *sefer*.

"Wow," said Kobi an hour later, "I never knew there were *dinim* about things like that. That's really neat. I won't forget it either. As soon as I finish *davening,* the colt and the mule get fed first!"

That afternoon, Kobi went to collect his first basket of pigeons' eggs. He didn't like collecting eggs as must as he liked feeding the pigeons. "I feel like a thief, taking their eggs away. They all make such a racket about it! One even poked me in the face!" complained Kobi.

When he told his Zaidy, he was in for another surprise. "Oh Kobi," he said, "you did something very wrong. Didn't you send the mother pigeons away before you took the eggs out of the nests?"

"No. I didn't think of it. Should I have?"

"Of course! Don't you know about *Shiluach hakan?* It's forbidden to take a wild bird's eggs out of the nest while the mother is sitting on them. You are supposed to send her away. This applies to all kosher wild birds.

"I think we'd better take a look at that *halachah* too," said Zaidy. And they did. Koby paid very strict attention to make sure he wouldn't forget!

The next day Kobi was working with his plow when he thought, "This thing works O.K., but what it needs is more horsepower — HEY ... I HAVE a horse! I'll harness the colt up together with the mule, and if they're BOTH pulling, I should be able to work a whole lot faster!"

But when Zaidy saw Kobi walking down the newly opened furrows behind the two animals, he called out sharply, "Kobi — take the colt off this minute!"

"But why?"

"Because it's forbidden to hitch up two different kinds of animals and work them together."

Then Kobi had more trouble with the mule. When the wheat started to come up, the mule would nibble away at the young shoots coming up through the ground. Kobi was rummaging through the barn looking for some sort of a muzzle to put on him. He asked Zaidy what he could use and the answer was,

"Sorry, Kobi. *Assur* (forbidden) again. If you are working an animal in the field, you can't muzzle him so he won't eat. You'll have to find a different solution. How about tying a feed bag on him so he can nibble when he feels like it without ruining your field. And it's back to the *seforim* to learn about it tonight!"

The first *Shabbos,* Kobi had thought, "At least today I won't make any more farming mistakes. It gives me a chance to relax a little. Zaidy sure keeps a fellow on his toes! I never knew it was so complicated to run a Torah farm!"

On *Shabbos* morning Kobi came down all dressed up and ready to go to shul in the morning. But there was Zaidy in coveralls. Kobi just gasped! "But Zaidy, it's SHABBOS!"

"Of course it is. But the cows have to be milked. They will be in terrible pain if we don't milk them for twenty-four hours. It's real *tzar baalei chaim* (pain of the animal). With milking machines, there is a special way we do it according to *halachah.* And we use an electric clock to turn on the machines, just as we set the lights in the house to go off and on.

"I'll be ready for shul soon, after I check the barns. Meanwhile you can look up some of the *halachos* about milking." All that day, Kobi learned about milking cows on *Shabbos.* It was then that Kobi made his GREAT DECISION FOR THE SUMMER: whether he would grow up to be a farmer or a rabbi, he had to become a *talmid chacham* (Torah scholar)!

So Kobi set up two regular study periods with his Zaidy — before work and after work. Suddenly, all areas of Torah study became more and more interesting.

When Kobi's parents came for a visit a few weeks later, Zaidy said to them, "You're in for quite a surprise. That boy has turned into a real scholar. When he opens a *sefer*, he's like a fish in water."

Abba was shocked. "Who, Kobi? But he wanted to come here to work, not to learn. What happened?"

Kobi grinned, showing all his dimples.

"I found out, Abba, that a Jew just can't get through the day and do anything right without learning Torah. And you know what else? I like it!"

The Prayer of Ovadyah the Sofer

by Rabbi Israel Kaminsky

Not so very long ago, there lived a little boy in a small Jewish village far, far away in the middle of the sands of Arabia. His name was Ezra.

One morning — of a day Ezra was always to remember — he sat at the edge of the little pool just outside the village and gazed into its waters. It was from this pool that the villagers drew the water for themselves, their goats, and their olive trees. They called the pool the Fountain of the Miracle. G-d, they said, wanted a village here, and so the waters from deep under the ground came bubbling up at His command.

As Ezra gazed into the pool, he wished that there would be another kind of a miracle. He wished that Hashem would make him well. For Ezra, you see, was a very sick little boy. His skin was all yellow and he was very weak. Ever since he became sick he did not care to eat, and he could not take many steps without wanting to lie down.

Whenever his parents would bring Ezra into the hut of the *Chacham* Menashe, the wise old rabbi would shake his head sadly. He had seen such sickness before. He had seen men, women and children grow weaker and weaker until they were no more. Sometimes, however, they did become better. The *Chacham* Menashe — and everyone else in the village — could only pray for little Ezra.

Ezra did not study *Torah* in the synagogue with the other children. The *moreh* (teacher) said that he was too weak for that and that he must rest until Hashem made him well. And so, every morning, when the children went to study *Torah,* Ezra would go the other way — to the pool — to look into the water to see if his face was still yellow. That is what Ezra was doing on the morning of this day that he was always to remember.

Ezra looked and looked at his face in the mirror of water. It was just as yellow as before — maybe even more yellow. Ezra felt like crying. Flies buzzed around him and bit him on his legs and the back of his neck, but he was too sad and weak to brush them off.

He heard the sound of children chanting *Chumash* in chorus. Then he heard the *moreh* rap with his pointer on the hard clay floor of the synagogue. A child had made a mistake, and the *moreh* stopped the chanting so that he could correct him. "Ah," thought Ezra, "how I would like to learn *Torah* — even with mistakes."

Then he thought of Ovadyah the *sofer* (scribe), who sat all day on the hill behind the village, writing a *Sefer Torah*. Ovadyah was a very old man with a beard as white as the fleece of little lambs. Each morning, he would go up the hill with his tiny worktable, his scrolls of parchment and a little sack in which he kept his quill-pen and ink and the bread and olives for his midday meal. He would sit cross-legged all day doing his holy work.

Ezra got up to go to the *sofer*. As fast as his weak legs could take him, he walked through the village and up the hill. He was out of breath when he reached the top of the hill. As soon as Ezra appeared, the old man, without even turning his head toward him, put his finger to his lips. It really wasn't necessary because Ezra knew that he mustn't say anything, as that would disturb the *sofer* and might cause him to make a mistake. He must only watch, and would be able to ask his questions later, when the old man stopped his writing to eat his midday meal.

Ezra sat down next to the *sofer*. Ovadyah always worked in the shadow of a big rock which stood right in the middle of the flat top of the hill. Of course, the shadow on the rock would move as the day went on. But Ovadyah would move himself and his table right along with the shadow. Only when the sun was low in the west and the shadow of the rock was very, very long, would Ovadyah roll up his scrolls and come back to the village.

Ezra watched the lines of Hebrew words appear as if by magic on the white parchment. "How beautiful Hebrew letters are!" he thought. Ezra loved to look at jewels — red ones and green ones and blue ones — but he thought that these black little letters that flowed from the quill-pen of Ovadyah the *sofer* were even more beautiful than jewels. Ezra watched for a long time until he became so weary that he lay down and stretched out on the cool earth. There was a question he wanted to ask Ovadyah, but he must wait until the old man stopped writing.

At last, the time of the midday meal arrived. Ovadyah turned and smiled down on Ezra.

"Ah, Ezra," he said, "so you have come to see to it that I do my work well!"

But Ezra's mind was bursting with the question he had wanted to ask all morning. "Ovadyah," he popped out, "when will you finish your *Sefer Torah?*"

Ovadyah put his arm under Ezra's shoulders and raised him, so that they sat side by side. "I am a very old man," he said, "and I don't think I will live long enough to finish it."

Ezra looked with surprise into the old man's eyes. "You will not finish the *Sefer Torah?*" he cried.

"No, little Ezra," sighed the old man, "Hashem wants us to do only what we can. Sometimes we can start something, but we must leave it for someone else to finish."

"But *who* will finish your *Torah?*" cried Ezra.

Ovadyah's arm tightened around the little boy. "Perhaps *you* will," he whispered.

A sad look came into Ezra's face, and he felt as bad as he did when he looked into the pool early that morning. "I ... I am sick," said Ezra in a downcast voice.

"Ah, Ezra," said the old man, looking kindly into the eyes of the little boy, "Hashem is merciful. I shall pray for you later, little Ezra." And as he said that, he lifted his face and rolled his eyeballs upward until Ezra could see almost nothing but the whites of his eyes.

At the end of the same day, Ovadyah the *sofer* was the *sh'liach tzibur (chazzan)* at the *Minchah* prayer. Ezra stood next to him as he recited the *Shemoneh Esrei* aloud for the congregation. The old man trembled and shook up and down as he prayed. Soon Ezra was shaking up and down together with him.

When Ovadyah came to the blessing, *Shma Koleinu* (Hear our voice), he began to tremble even more, and when he finished the blessing with the words Blessed are You, Hashem who hears our prayers, he closed his eyes so tightly and gave his head such a hard shake to the side that Ezra looked at him in amazement.

That night, Ezra dreamed a strange dream. Ovadyah the *sofer* was holding the scroll of his unfinished Torah close to his heart, and was dancing with it slowly toward Ezra. A tear rolled down the old man's cheek and onto his beard. But when he saw Ezra, he smiled, and his face was full of happiness. Then he held out the scroll for Ezra to take.

When Ezra woke up in the morning, his mother was staring down at him, her eyes wide open, as if she were seeing something unbelievable. She tried to speak, but she couldn't. She just stood there, pointing a trembling finger at Ezra.

Ezra's father jumped out of bed, and as he looked at his little boy, he cried out, "*Baruch Hashem* (Blessed is Hashem)!" And, suddenly, Ezra knew what had happened.

Yes, Ezra's face was no longer yellow. His cheeks were red with health, and his dark eyes sparkled with life. He leaped up and flew into the arms of his mother, who hugged him tightly and cried with happiness.

A few minutes later, the news was all over the village — and what a celebration there was! People crowded into the hut, then brought Ezra outside, lifted him in the air and danced and sang. Sa'adyah the silversmith came running with the pair of cymbals he used for weddings and other joyous occasions. The men danced to the clangings of Sa'adyah's cymbals, and the women raised their hands to their mouths and let out loud warbling shrieks. This, they say, keeps the evil eye of Satan from looking at a happy thing and spoiling it.

Above the joyous noise of the shrieking and singing, somebody suddenly shouted, "The *Chacham* Menashe is not here! We must bring the *Chacham!*" And a man ran out from the crowd to find the *Chacham* and tell him the wonderful news.

But the *Chacham* Menashe was not in his hut. And the man could not find him anywhere else. Finally, he looked toward the hill of Ovadyah the *sofer*, and there, on top of the hill, was the *Chacham* standing alone with his head bowed.

The man ran up the hill and shouted "Oh *Chacham*, *Chacham!* A miracle has happened! The sickness of little Ezra is gone!"

The *Chacham* looked up and smiled. "Yes, I know," he said. "Praised be Hashem." Then he lowered his head again.

"But why do you look down at the earth so sadly?" asked the man.

"Blessed is Hashem, the True Judge," said the *Chacham* in a low and trembling voice.

These solemn words are said when a person dies. The man looked up in surprise.

"Ovadyah the *sofer*," added the *Chacham*, "has passed away in his sleep."

All this, dear children, happened almost fifty years ago. Today, Ezra is a grown and married man, and lives on a farm settlement in Israel. Each evening, after he has come in from the fields and eaten his supper, he sits down to the work he loves best of all. If his children come into the room while he is doing this work, he puts his finger to his lips so that they should not disturb him. For Ezra is now a *sofer*.

When he grew up, he finished Ovadyah's *Sefer Torah,* and since then he has written hundreds of *mezuzos, tefillin,* and Torah scrolls.

Double-header in Grahamsville

by Sheindel Weinbach

It was only a quarter to eight in the morning, but the July sun was hot on Yossi Friedman's neck as he raced up Maple Street on his old bicycle. He noticed his friend Sammy on the sidewalk and waved to him.

"Hey, Yossi!" called Sammy. "We're having an early game at the empty lot this morning. Can you come down now?"

"I can't," answered Yossi. "I've got to find someone for a *minyan* (ten men, the quorum for prayers) in *shul.*"

"*Minyan, shminyan.* You're always running errands for those old men in *shul.* Go play ball with them," sneered Sammy. "We'll get a game together without you."

For a second Yossi felt like abandoning his errand and joining Sammy, but he promptly forgot about it when he saw Mr. Rosen at his window a few houses down. He called to him and asked if he could come to *shul* that day, as they needed just one more man for the *minyan.*

"Sure thing, Yossi. I was going to *daven* (pray) at home, because I thought I was late. But if they still need me I'll be there right away."

Yossi made a U-turn and pedaled back to *shul*, his mission accomplished. He went inside and took out his own *tefillin* and started putting them on for the second time in his life. He put the square *tefillin* on his left arm and he felt his fingers curve automatically around an imaginary ball. "Who cares anyway," thought Yossi. "I'm going to be *Bar Mitzvah* in a month and then I won't have so much time for games. Anyway, with me included, we'll be 10% closer to a *minyan*, and we'll be able to *daven* earlier."

Yossi looked around and saw everyone *davening* quietly. Everyone — but that wasn't much, just the ten older men and himself.

Grahamsville, Ohio, had only a handful of religious Jews and very often they couldn't even scrape together a *minyan*. It was Yossi's job to look for the tenth man every morning, and in return for his efforts, Mr. Rubinstein, the *shammos* (caretaker), would review Yossi's *Bar Mitzvah sidrah* with him and teach him some *Chumash* and *Rashi*. Since there was no yeshivah in Grahamsville, he depended on his daily two-hour sessions with Mr. Rubinstein — mornings in the summer and after school in the winter — for his Jewish education. Mr. Friedman, Yossi's father, had promised to let Yossi go to yeshivah high school in a nearby city after his *Bar Mitzvah*. Yossi could hardly wait. There he would make some new friends — not the boys like Sammy who could think only of two things: playing ball and watching ball games on T.V. — but boys who also appreciated studying Torah and keeping its *mitzvos*.

Yossi reviewed all these thoughts in his mind after the *davening*, as he carefully put his *tefillin* back into the new blue velvet sack.

The two-hour study session slipped by quickly, and Yossi went outside to hop onto his bike and go home. He looked his bike over carefully, and noticed the kickstand giving way. The front fender was missing when his cousin gave it to him, and the back fender did not last much longer. Yossi's long legs hardly had room to pedal this ancient 24-incher back home.

"It can't last me much longer," he told his mother during his late breakfast.

"I know, dear, but we can't afford a new one now that we're saving every penny for yeshivah," Mrs. Friedman replied with a sigh.

"Right, Ma. I didn't mean to complain. I guess I'll manage until September."

After lunch Yossi went riding around, looking for something to do. He passed the empty lot and saw the game going on, but both teams were filled up. Sammy, in the outfield, saw him and shouted something, but Yossi was glad he could not hear him since he was probably calling him some kind of name.

Yossi rode on to the downtown section. He looked at the store windows as he rode along.

"Hi there, Yossi," he heard someone calling. "Could you please bring this package over to 201 Elm St. for me?"

It was Mr. Rosen, whom he had called to *minyan* in the morning.

"Sure thing," Yossi said. "You came to *shul* for me, so why shouldn't I do this for you?"

Mr. Rosen laughed. "I really came to *shul* for myself — and if you do a good job on this delivery, I'll let you handle all my errands for a salary, plus tips. How's that for *you?*"

That was how Yossi started working for Rosen's Dry Goods — running errands, delivering, and even selling when Mr. Rosen was very busy. The dime and quarter tips and the two-dollars-a-day wages started to add up and it was then that Yossi decided to save up for a new ten-speed bike.

The summer days flew by quickly for Yossi, for he was busy learning and working. On Sunday afternoons Mr. Friedman would plan something special to relieve the strain of the busy schedule. Once Mr. Friedman got three tickets to a Reds' ball-game in Cincinnati. Yossi decided to invite Sammy although they had not spoken much to each other since that day in the beginning of July.

"Boy, that'd be great," said Sammy shyly when he was asked. "I'll be over right after breakfast. It's a long trip to Cincinnati."

Sammy was so excited that he came to the Friedman house at 7:30

in the morning. He met Yossi and his father on the doorstep, leaving for *shul*.

"We can't miss *minyan* today. Someone has *Yahrtzeit* (anniversary of a death)," said Yossi, and started explaining what that meant. "Come along. No one is going to bite you."

The *shammos* met them at the door of the *shul*.

"Good morning, Mr. Friedman. Hello Yossi … Let's see now. You make eight, and Yossi's still too young. We need two more people."

"I'll find someone," volunteered Yossi. "Come on, Sammy. It won't take long."

They went over to Mr. Cohen's house, since he was the nearest person they could think of.

"I wish I could go," Mr. Cohen said, "But I have no one to watch little Mendy. His mother is in the hospital with our newborn daughter."

"We could stay here and watch him," suggested Sammy.

"But we still wouldn't have ten people," said Yossi. "Who else could we try?"

"I'm thirteen already," said Sammy. "I know how to *daven* a little. Do you think there's an extra pair of *tefillin* in *shul*? I-m-uh-m-don't have mine with me."

"Sure, just ask Mr. Rubinstein — he'll give you a pair, and then you'll be the tenth man."

Mr. Cohen and Sammy hurried away together, leaving Yossi with Mendy, who was napping. Yossi *davened* in Mr. Cohen's house, but with more *kavanah* (thought) than usual. He prayed that Sammy would change his opinion about religious matters after this morning in *shul*.

After forty minutes Yossi heard voices down the block. Through the window he saw Sammy walking between Mr. Friedman and Mr. Cohen, talking excitedly.

"I never thought there were so many interesting things to know about being a Jew," he explained later in the car, on the way to Cincinnati. "It's not old-man stuff at all."

Yossi and his father spoke to Sammy, trying to convince him to join Yossi in his daily lessons with the *shammos*. Sammy agreed to come once in a while.

The game that afternoon was very exciting, but strangely enough on the way home Sammy was still asking about *tefillin*, *Sifrei Torah*, *davening*, and *minyan*.

Sammy and Yossi became good friends after that. Yossi asked Sammy to come to *shul* on the *Shabbos* of his *Bar Mitzvah* to hear him read the *sidrah*. He also asked him to join his family on Sunday, when the Friedmans had an open house in his honor.

❀ ❀ ❀

On Sunday, many guests came bringing gifts with them. Yossi opened them and thanked everyone. Then he announced, "Since I'm going away to yeshivah, I decided that I really don't need a bike any more. I took the money I saved and bought a present for Sammy, who never had a real *Bar Mitzvah*."

"You're crazy," said Sammy with tears in his eyes, as he accepted the square package and started to open it. He took the paper off the package, and removed the lid from the cardboard box. Inside was a red velvet bag.

"Why, it's a brand new pair of *tefillin* — all my own!" whispered Sammy. "Now I can go to *shul*, and not have to borrow someone else's."

Sammy's father spoke up. "We also got *you* something, Yossi. I work for the department store downtown and I was able to get this for you at a big discount."

He then wheeled a new ten-speed bike into the room.

"We have another surprise for you, too," he said to the speechless Yossi. "Sammy has convinced me to send him to yeshivah with you this fall."

The rest of the day Yossi went around in a daze. A new bike of his own! A friend to go to yeshivah with him! And not just anyone — but Sammy whom he was working on all summer! He hardly remembered going to sleep that night. He awoke the next morning and opened his eyes to his new bike — for his mother had let him keep it in his room for that night. He took it outside, put his *tefillin* bag in the basket, and rode to *shul.*

"Today's your day, Yossi my boy," greeted the *Shammos.*

"What do you mean, Mr. Rubinstein? I was *Bar Mitzvah* on *Shabbos,* don't you remember?" he said to the old man.

"I know, Yossele, but today is still your day. Today you are the tenth man for the *minyan.*"

Proud of his important new role — completing the *minyan* himself this time, instead of by getting someone else — Yossi strode over to his regular seat in *shul.* His father was already there, wearing his *tallis* and *tefillin,* and he nodded to Yossi. On the other side of his seat was Sammy, too engrossed in putting on his new pair of *tefillin* even to notice that Yossi had walked in. Mr. Rubinstein had made an error. It was also Sammy's day in the Grahamsville *shul* ... It was a real double-header.

Grandfather and the Rain

*A story told by Yeminite Jews
retold by Rabbi Charles Wengrov*

For the boy or girl in the city, rain isn't much fun. Usually, it means no playing out-of-doors, and putting on rubbers and raincoat; and many times it causes colds. But to the farmer, the man who grows food on his land, rain is tremendously important. If there were no rain, the farmer's crops would wither and die; no plants would grow, and soon there would be a shortage of food. That is why Jews pray regularly for rainfall.

This is a story of what happened when rain didn't fall for more than a year over the land of Teiman (Yemen), a small country at the southern tip of the Arabian peninsula. The Jews of Teiman say this story happened almost a hundred fifty years ago.

> *It happened that when* Eretz Yisrael *needed rain, the Rabbis asked a great tzaddik named* Choni *to pray. What did he do? He made a circle in the sand and stood inside it; and he said, "Master of the universe, Your children have turned to me, for I am near to You. I swear by Your great name that I will not leave this circle until You will have mercy on Your children." It began to drizzle very slightly. Said Choni, "Not for this did I pray, but for rain to fill all the wells and reservoirs." Suddenly, it began to pour furiously, and it seemed that there would soon be a damaging flood. Said Choni, "Not for this did I pray, but for a good, kindly, blessed rain." The rain became steady and moderate. Because of that story, people called him* Choni HaMe'agel *(the Circle Maker).* — Talmud Taanis, 19a

"Mother, may I have another piece of bread?" I asked plaintively. "I'm so hungry."

Mother patted my cheek. "I know you are, dear," she said. "But if you eat any more today you won't have enough tomorrow. It's hard for you, I know. But everyone is hungry. You must be brave."

Father came into the room then. "Are you ready to go to the

synagogue?" he asked. "Let's go. Grandfather is there already."

It happened so many years ago, yet I remember it clearly even today. I close my eyes, and I can see myself walking to the synagogue with Mother and Father. When we arrived we saw Grandfather, his beard all white, standing by the building.

You see, there was famine in the land of Teiman. Famine means no food, and no food means hunger. For over a year no rain had fallen, and I remember how the wheat and corn looked all shriveled and dry in the nearby fields. Hardly any fruit grew on the trees. Along the streets of our city, there used to be all kinds of fruit stands, but now they were gone.

And all because there was no rain. For over a year the sun beat down mercilessly day after day, and the farmland became hard, baked. Without rain, nothing could grow. That was why we had only bread and water. Whatever food could be bought cost enormous sums of money.

And the Jews of Teiman were poor.

What do you do to bring rain? You pray. Every afternoon we all went to the synagogue, men, women, and children. From there we marched through the streets. Every man wore a *tallis* and *tefillin*. At our head, the rabbi and a few others carried *Sifrei Torah* (scrolls). We chanted *Tehillim* (Psalms), and many shed bitter tears and cried aloud. We knew that if rain didn't fall soon, we would starve to death.

The sun beat down fiercely; it was unbearably hot. I was in the back with my friends, and we chanted the Psalms too. Even we children knew it was important. Then, as every day, we met the Arab procession. The Moslem Arabs also marched through the streets every afternoon, praying in their own fashion, and every day we passed each other. Suddenly, all praying stopped, and both groups, Moslems and Jews, stood still. An Arab had climbed up on a high flat rock, and he began shouting. We all turned to listen. He shouted with all his might.

"Listen, my friends. Do you want to know who is to blame for our hunger? The Jews — no one else. I tell you, they can bring rain whenever they want. There is a story they tell from the time they lived in Palestine and had their Temple. They needed rain, just as we do now. One of their learned, pious men took a stick and made a circle in the sand around himself, and he said, 'Almighty Master, I will not leave this circle until You give us rain.' That's all he did, and soon rain fell. Ask the Jews if it isn't true. Go ahead, ask them. *They* know the story. *Choni HaMe'agel,* they call him, Choni the Circle-Maker." The Arab was almost screaming. I pushed forward to see him better.

"I tell you, my friends," he shouted on, waving his arms wildly, "the power to bring rain is given to the Jews. In every generation there is at least one Jew who can make it rain whenever he wants to. But these Jews of Teiman do not want to. They would rather *starve,* as long as we hunger, too. Do you think it is natural that no rain has fallen for a whole year? This is *their* doing, I tell you. Let us go to the king and make him issue a decree: Either the Jews bring rain, or they die."

The Arabs certainly agreed with him. I couldn't see any proof for what he said, but the Arabs drank in every word, for they were eager to find a scapegoat — someone or something to blame for their hunger. We saw three Moslems set out for the palace. We lived in the capital city of Teiman, and the palace was only ten minutes away from us. Our people stood there, afraid to do anything. The Moslem on the rock kept shouting the same thing over and over.

Less than an hour later the three Moslems were back, waving a piece of paper excitedly. They handed it to their friend on the rock, and he read it in triumph.

"Be it known that the Jews of Teiman must bring rain in the next three days. If they fail, they are to be killed."

The Arabs began talking excitedly, all at once; they were overjoyed. We separated and went home. None of us smiled.

That night I couldn't sleep. I tossed and turned on my bed. And all the while I heard Grandfather chanting prayers softly. His voice was so sad … heartbreaking … I looked up through my window at the sky. The moon and the stars shone clearly, and for once I hated them. I prayed in my heart that big, black clouds should come, and bring rain.

We spent the next three days in the synagogue, fasting and praying. It was like *Yom Kippur,* but the crying was more fervent than on that holy day. The third day everything was the same, until Grandfather went up to the rabbi late in the afternoon and asked permission to lead the *Minchah* (afternoon) prayers. That was strange, for Grandfather had never led any service before. But even more strange were his eyes. They seemed to shine, and I thought they were seeing far beyond our vision, reading the future. And when he prayed there wasn't a dry eye in the place.

Minchah was over. And then Grandfather did his second strange thing. He asked everyone to go outside. We all gathered in the street; then he came out. He looked like an angel from heaven then. The people drew back before him. And in his hand was a stick! I halfguessed what was coming …

In the sand of the street he drew, slowly and carefully, a circle around himself with the stick. Then he turned his eyes to heaven. The sun was setting in the west, and its last gold-red rays shone on him. He then spoke, quietly and gently; we were still, listening eagerly to every word. To my dying day I'll remember those words.

Grandfather and the Rain / 75

"Master of the universe, do You want Your children to die? All our lives we try to obey Your commands, no matter how hard they are. We do not cheat; we do not steal. The scales we use to weigh the things we

sell are correct; we never cheat, for so do You command us. It is hard for us to earn a living, but we struggle, for it is Your will. We beg You, have mercy on us. It is so easy for You to send rain."

He paused, and the silence hung heavy. The sun had sunk a little further down toward the west.

"I am no *Choni HaMe'agel,* O Father in Heaven. I have not his piety or his wisdom. But Your children are in danger, and I cannot be still." And now he raised his voice and shouted, "Master of the universe, I swear before You: I do not leave this circle until rain falls. Almighty G-d, here I stay until You have mercy on Your children."

Now all was still again. The people stood silent, waiting ... waiting for I knew not what. The sun was setting now. Toward the west the sky was inflamed with purple and gold light. Then someone whispered, "Look, isn't that a cloud? There, toward the north." The whisper was like a shot in the deep silence, and everyone looked northward. Clouds were rolling in, faster than I'd ever seen clouds travel. They came and came, until the last light of the sun was darkened. And then lightning tore across the sky, and thunder boomed. By the flashes of lightning I saw Grandfather; he stood perfectly still in his circle. Only his lips moved ... And then I felt the first drop.

I tell you, I've lived almost eighty years; never again have I felt as I felt then, when the first drops of rain touched my face.

The people went crazy with joy. They began to dance and sing and shout. People were embracing and kissing each other. You would have thought they had gone quite mad, doing all that while the rain poured down faster and faster. But I didn't stay there. I had to run with my family to help — Grandfather had fainted.

That is the story of my grandfather and the rain. It only remains for me to add that the Jews of the city insisted on making Grandfather assistant rabbi, and the king made him a royal advisor, and consulted him on all kinds of problems. After this we had rain quite often; and by the next *Tu B'Sh'vat* there were gay stands again, selling all kinds of fruit.

Songs of Praise

by Ruth Finkelstein

I t was a golden late-afternoon of early September and Naftali was on his way to shul for *Minchah* (afternoon service). The truth was that deep down he was still somewhat annoyed at having had to stop working on his model airplane in order to go to *daven*. Not that he didn't like to *daven;* oh, no! He just didn't like to be interrupted when he was doing something he enjoyed very much.

Now he was half walking, half running along the asphalt road that led through the little town where he was visiting his aunt for a few days before school started. He stopped only long enough to kick the pebble that he was propelling ahead of him down the road to *shul*.

Thus he ran-walked with his right hand firmly in his right jacket pocket, and his eyes squinting after the little stone as it sailed through the air and then came bouncing down with a plinkety, plink, plink — plink. The reason his hand was in his pocket was because he was tightly holding on to his pocket *siddur* there to make sure that he wouldn't lose it "by accident," as happened sometimes with other things that "somehow fell out of my pocket." A *siddur* is sacred, however, and must be handled properly, Naftali knew.

Presently, several wildly screaming bluejays drew Naftali's attention to a cluster of young trees to the right of the road. He stopped, at a safe distance, and watched with fascination as the furious birds, still shrieking, swooped down again and again trying to get a peck at the offender. Naftali tried to make out in the tall grass what animal the jays were after. But try as he might all he could glimpse was a swiftly fleeing patch of grey fur as it disappeared in a clump of thick shrubbery.

The bluejays refused to give up. They rushed the opening into which the furry creature had vanished. The animal continued its terror-stricken flight on the other side of the low bushes, with the jays in hot pursuit.

Now Naftali was even more curious to see what animal would abandon a safe hide-out and let itself be hounded that way. He bolted around the bushes and started after the chase that was now zig-zagging through the woods. Now this way, now that, deeper and deeper into the woods they went: furry animal, bluejays — and Naftali, until they reached a clearing. There Naftali caught up with the noisy birds — but the little creature had escaped.

Out of breath, Naftali sat down on a rock to rest. After a while, the bluejays ceased their ear-piercing noise, and Naftali watched one of the birds alight on a nearby tree with an acorn in its beak. It placed the acorn securely between its feet, cracked the shell with a few sharp taps of its strong beak, and ate the nut. Then it cleaned its beak by rubbing it a few times from side to side against the branch on which it was perched.

What Naftali saw next brought to his mind something his *rebbi* of the previous school year had mentioned: Naftali noticed that the bluejay, after it had finished cleaning its beak, stood stock-still for a moment and then took off into the sunlight with a loud jubilant note. It says in *Tehillim* (Psalms), the *rebbi* had said, that all living things daily sing *shirah* (song) in praise of *Hashem*. Could it be, wondered Naftali, that the bird's still moment and its cry of joy had been its way of praising *Hashem* and thanking Him for the acorn?

Luckily, *shirah* and saying thanks to *Hashem* reminded Naftali that he was supposed to be on his way to *shul* for *Minchah* and *Maariv* (evening service). He checked his watch; it was already time for *Minchah*. So he pulled his pocket *siddur* from his pocket and *davened* right then and there.

Now, with the last sun rays stealing over the horizon, Naftali had about twenty minutes to get to *shul* in time for *Maariv*. He set off at a full run into the woods, zig-zagging in and out between the trees toward the road. Soon he would see the black-top road glistening in the sunset through the trees. But where was it? Breathing heavily and with a sinking feeling in his stomach, Naftali ran off in another direction only to come out on the other side of the same clearing. He realized that he had traveled in a wide half-circle and — that he was lost.

Naftali's aunt, Tante Rayzel, had prepared supper and set the table. A widow living alone, she didn't often have somone to eat with, so she looked forward to her nephew's arrival for supper. "Any moment now," she thought, as she checked the clock and went to sit by the front window to watch for him.

A half-hour passed and she became uneasy. *Maybe Naftali stopped to talk or play with some of the boys in the neighborhood.* Another half-hour ticked by. *What's keeping him? Why didn't he at least call?* Another half-hour. *Who knows? Maybe a car or ...* She stopped herself from thinking further and bustled to the phone.

"Rabbi Sofer? ... This is Mrs. Green ... Did you see who Naftali left *shul* with after *Maariv* or where he went? ... You didn't see him altogether!? ... He wasn't in *shul?* Thanks. Yes, I'll let you know."

"Hello, Feivel. Is Naftali at your house? Do you know where he is? You didn't see him altogether!? ... *Vei is mir ...*"

"Captain Smith, this is Mrs. Green. My nephew is missing ... He left the house at 6:30 tonight to go to evening services, and no one has seen him there or since ... Naftali Dembowitz ... ten, I think, maybe eleven ... about 4½ feet tall ... brown hair ... brown eyes ... brown pants, olive green jacket ..."

Mrs. Green hung up, wrung her hands and began to cry. Then she straightened as though she had taken new hope. She got up and went for her *Sefer Tehillim* (Psalms): *"Ya'ancha Hashem b'yom tzara* (Hashem will answer you in your day of trouble)."

❋ ❋ ❋

Naftali had *davened Maariv* by moonlight and was now seated on a mound of earth in the clearing, his face buried in his knees and his arms wrapped around his head and legs. He was trying to keep out the nippy cold, to keep the insects from biting his face, and to block out the night-time sounds of rustling leaves and crackling branches. Nightfall brought him visions of wolves and bears on the hunt. Try as he might, he could not keep out the unbroken, high-pitched chirping and trilling of crickets and other insects. Just as *Hashem* takes care of all, even these tiny creatures, Naftali thought, so He will surely take care of me also. And then, almost as if on their own, his lips began to move as he recited psalms that he knew by heart from *Shacharis*: "*Somech Hashem l'chol hanoflim v'zokeif l'chol hakefufim* (Hashem supports all the fallen ones and straightens all the hunched) … *Korov Hashem l'chol kor'ov, l'chol asher yikro'uhu ve'emes*" (Hashem is close to all who call upon Him — to all who call upon Him sincerely).

"*Hallelukah!* Proclaim *Hashem's* praise … from the earth, species of fish and all swirling floods … fire and hail, snow and vapor, stormy wind, fulfilling His word … mountains and all hills, fruit trees and all cedars … beasts and all cattle, creeping things and winged fowl ... they will proclaim The Name of the L-rd ...

"*Kol haneshomo tehalel koh, Hallelukah!* (Let every breath of life proclaim *Hashem* through the praise of His mighty acts: *Hallelukah!)*"

Word for word, with tears in his eyes, over and over again, Naftali prayed until he finally fell fast asleep.

The next morning, Naftali awoke with a start. Where was he? He felt chilled and damp and very hungry. His heart sank as he remembered that he was lost. The crisp early-morning air was so full of the fragrance of blossoms and grass that he couldn't resist taking several deep breaths. That and the brilliant sunshine made him feel a little better.

He lay back and listened to the early-morning symphony of nature's musicians: the chirping, trilling, whistling, buzzing, ticking and chattering of birds, insects and little animals plus the whispering of the wind through the nearby treetops. As a city boy, he could identify but few of nature's voices. Nonetheless, they had a soothing effect on him.

Not long ago he had heard a nature talk in which the speaker said that we can often tell what an animal is expressing by the kind of sound it makes. A dog's sudden, short yelp is usually its way of showing sudden pain, or "Ouch, it hurts!" A cat's purring is its way of saying, "I'm contented." But there are times, the naturalist had said, when animals seem to make sounds, like dogs barking or birds chirping or squirrels chattering, just for the sake of "talking," as if they were simply trying to say, "I'm glad to be alive!"

Naftali wondered if what the naturalists called "joy-of-living sounds" weren't really the animals saying *shirah* to Hashem. For it says in *Tehillim* (148:10), "*Ha'chayah vechol behemah remes vetzipor kanaf ... yehalelu es sheim Hashem ...* (beasts and all cattle, creeping things and winged fowl ... they will proclaim the Name of *Hashem*)."

Who could know?

The chop-chop of a helicopter jolted Naftali from his musings. As if propelled by a spring, he jumped to his feet and waved his arms excitedly. But the helicopter flew by without a sign of recognition. "How stupid of me," sobbed Naftali. "How could anybody see me in the woods when I'm wearing brown pants and a green jacket?" Off came the jacket, but the helicopter was already far away.

Naftali cried as he hadn't cried since he was a little boy. Then he washed as best as he could with the dew from the grass, and started to *daven Shacharis*. There it was again, the chopping of the helicopter! Naftali waved his bare arms wildly, jumping up and down and shouting at the top of his lungs. As the helicopter began circling overhead, Naftali ripped off his shirt, pulled of his *tallis koton (tzitzis),* and vigorously waved it like a flag to signal the helicopter.

As Naftali wildly waved his *tzitzis* flag, hoping the helicopter could see him, the pilot of the whirly-bird was calling in to headquarters.

"We found him, he is jumping up and down waving something white. We'll go down and try to bring him up on the rescue ladder. If that doesn't work, we will lead a rescue party through the woods. Over."

The helicopter dropped down until it seemed to be sitting on the tree tops. It hovered there and lowered its ladder. The co-pilot scrambled down to help Naftali up. As he entered the cockpit, Naftali whispered his thanks to *Hashem*. The pilot picked up his radio-telephone and said, "Thank G-d, we got him. He is all right." As the helicopter rose above the earth, the birds below continued their song, the insects their humming, and the squirrels their chattering; Naftali, too, sang a silent song of thanks to *Hashem* for saving his life. And as the helicopter rose higher and higher, so did Naftali's whispered and heartfelt words, as the wind picked them up and brought them over the clouds and into the heavens straight to the throne of *Hashem*.

A Message from the Man on the Moon

by Rabbi Zevulun Weisberger

On that bright July morning near the end of the century, the three astronauts walked down the path to the space vehicle. A few photographers waved, and they waved back. The space trips seemed so natural now that dozens of space flights to the moon had been completed successfully. Times had changed since the 1960's and 70's when such flights had been big news all over the world. Now, not as many people took notice of such flights, and they had become routine.

David Gordon was thrilled, however. One does not travel to the moon every day. True, he had felt disappointed at not being chosen first for an earlier celestial adventure, but the excitement of the moment overshadowed his earlier frustrations.

The astronauts awaited the countdown. David started to reflect on his personal role in this undertaking, and his mood changed again. Throughout his life, he always strove for a "first" — some great accomplishment for which he could be remembered. Very few humans had ever gone to the moon, it is true, but David was just one member of the American crew to be stationed on the moon for two months, to be replaced by a Russian group at the end of that period. That's how it had been set up by the International Space Agency —

American and Russian crews took turns manning a space station. People had forgotten the earlier group and probably would never take note of David and his mates on the Lunar V. There was one "first" for him, though. David was the first Jewish astronaut! And not only was he Jewish, he was an observant Jew!

The countdown began. David's spacemates, Duke Vance and Peter McKain, were tense, but confident. "We know quite a bit about the moon already. After every trip, more and more information is conveyed to scientists on earth, collected and digested. With all the computer printouts we've studied, we could write a book about it already," remarked Vance.

"Do you fellows realize something odd? Nothing spectacular has been learned since the first few landings!" declared McKain. "And all the details that have been added to the files — well, it's been interesting, but hardly moon-shaking."

"Well, we'll see for ourselves," said Gordon. "The experience itself should still be tremendous."

It was. The liftoff went smoothly and the spacecraft shot upwards. Their upward thrust out of earth's protective air blanket was like riding a bullet out of the barrel of a gun. The tremendous noise, the flash of light, the slow upward movement of the spacecraft, and then the steady pickup in speed never failed to thrill the onlookers, or David Gordon either. After the clearing of the trail of exhaust vapor, he looked around to see Houston, the State of Texas, and all of the Gulf of Mexico shrink behind them.

The astronauts reported all systems working perfectly and activated the retrorockets. After one complete spin around the home planet, they would go out of the atmosphere and into space. They watched the setting sun paint a red strip across Israel, Arabia, and the Indian Ocean. A few points in the vast darkness of the earthly night sparkled with the lights of the great cities of the East.

The sun rose over the blue Pacific Ocean that grew smaller and smaller by the minute. "Funny," thought David, "I davened *Shacharis* only four hours ago and I'm seeing another sunrise."

The rockets re-aligned the massive space ship with its ultimate target, the moon. Its guidance system pointed toward the spot where the moon would be in just another day and a half. Again the crew looked behind them, and watched the earth in the glorious blue of outer space. Now it looked almost as if it were just another heavenly body. Tiny meteorites whizzed by as the ship accelerated to 20,000 miles per hour, 25,000 miles per hour, and then an incredible 30,000 MPH!

"*Mah rabbu ma'asecha Hashem!* How Great are Thy works, O L-rd!!!" exclaimed Gordon. His companions stared at him but said nothing.

Darkness never arrived, for they were travelling on a dawn-line, yet the space travelers were required to rest so they would be ready for "tomorrow's" strenuous schedule of activities. Until they came near the moon, there would be very few duties on the agenda.

Gordon reflected a while. Maybe there would be a "first" on his trip. There was definitely something lacking in all the scientific reports of the previous missions — something basic.

Lunar V continued on its way. Vance broke the silence, "Do you think we'll be alert enough for the mission? I can't sleep my allotted four hours even with that sleeping pill I took."

"No reason for concern," Gordon said. "It's that first-night-in-space excitement. They warned us about it at control, and it's very true. Besides, we're in G-d's hands. He's here as well as on earth. He'll take care of us. I can't help feeling something special here — what about you?

McKain hesitated. "Well, it really is awesome out there," he finally said. "It makes me think that one never fully realizes how vast and breathtaking the universe really is."

"We have to broadcast a message to earth when we arrive. Do you fellows have any idea what we should say?" asked Vance.

"I wonder," Gordon mused. "Every mission broadcasts a message, but I think they miss the boat. They make scientific comments, or try some poetry, but they omit the obvious."

They were interrupted with a message from Earth Control Headquarters. The time had arrived for another rest period. Tomorrow was D-Day.

"The rabbi outlined a davening schedule for me in line with the Houston Time Zone. He gave me a special *Tefillas Haderech* (prayer said during dangerous journeys) for the space trip," Gordon thought, "but he neglected to suggest something for the arrival. There must be something special to say when arriving on another heavenly body, some special *Shehecheyanu* — a real big one!"

"Just imagine, Dave," Vance said, laughing. "You can build the first synagogue on the moon — you can even be the first rabbi there!"

David Gordon grinned. A shul was not included among the structures they were to erect, but it would be a nice idea ...

❈ ❈ ❈

D-day arrived. Signals from the Russian camp on the moon were picked up. Preparations for landing were made.

The tension and excitement of the landing itself was indescribable. The ship slowed until it seemed to hover over the gray, rocky surface of the moon. Then it slowly dropped and the astronauts held their breath, waiting for touchdown.

The moon did not seem to be an *enemy* of life. It seemed absolutely indifferent, as if it didn't care at all. What an inviting place earth seemed by comparison! Even the driest, sandiest desert on earth seemed more inviting. The landing legs dropped down and made contact with the lunar surface. The latch opened automatically. They had landed safely! They opened the hatch, dropped the ladder, and climbed gingerly down. How light they felt in the moon's gravity — even with their load of heavy equipment..

The exhausted but happy astronauts walked slowly about. The many craters yawned forebodingly in all directions, like Swiss cheese. A deep stillness covered the moonscape, and the lack of atmosphere lent

unusual visibility to the view. Contact had not yet been made with the space station on the far end of the landing area, but it seemed only a few jumps away.

The earth seemed like an immense half-moon in the center of the heaven. The dark half of earth lost its outline against an endless sky and the bright half was partly shrouded in pink and silver, reflecting the sun's rays. It was a stupendous sight.

"Gordon, you've got the gift of gab. How about conveying the message home? The people back on earth must be awaiting word of our landing. And I'm sure our wives and kids are anxious to know how we feel," Vance said.

"C'mon, Dave," urged McKain. "Let 'em know we're here."

The equipment was assembled and Gordon spoke into the sensitive mike.

"Attention, America! We have arrived safely on the moon, thank

G-d! I wish you could have been with us on our journey through the heavens for you would have understood for the first time the meaning of the Biblical passage: 'Hashamayim mesaprim kevod Keil, umaasei Yadav maggid harakiyah (The skies relate the glory of G-d, and the heavens tell the work of His hands)'. You have been flooded with statistics, pictures, and reports about the moon's surface, its craters, its texture, its atmosphere, its minerals, and its gravitational pull and luminosity. But they omitted the most vital fact of all — nowhere else can we recognize G-d's work more clearly — the amazing order of the heavenly bodies, the great universal structure created and guided by His powerful hand. All other facts are secondary to that great truth!"

"You'll go down in history," Vance smiled after the broadcast, "as the first man who really looked with two eyes wide open, the first man who noticed and proclaimed the obvious."

Gordon was not answering. The sun had just set on Houston, so he was busy davening *Minchah* — another "first" on the moon.

The Tarnished Penny

Adapted by Sheindel Weinbach

The drunken Russian general looked up from his couch at the simple but dignified Jew who stood in the doorway.

"Who let you in here?" he growled.

Reb Mendel, who had not been stopped by vicious dogs and armed soldiers that guarded the headquarters from trespassers, was determined to have the general hear what he had to say.

"Your soldiers who grab Jewish boys for the Czar's army have today snatched away a bridegroom from our village on the day of his wedding. I have come to buy him back."

The general's lips curled in a sneer as he spat out his words. "You dirty, beggarly Jews are always coming to me for petty favors! Why, I'll have you thrown to the dogs."

"Guard!" he shouted, as he picked up his glass of vodka and drained it.

"Wait," begged Reb Mendel. "We are willing to pay any price for this boy. He is an orphan and his bride also has no parents. Name your price and I guarantee you shall have it by tonight."

The general stomped up to Reb Mendel and, pointing to the door, snarled, "All right. Five thousand rubles by tonight, but don't come begging to me for leniency. Out! Away with you!"

Reb Mendel left the general's quarters and walked quickly back to his village, confident that Hashem Father of Orphans, would have pity and send the enormous sum to them — somehow.

He rushed to the house where Reb Levi Yitzchok, a *tzaddik* of world renown, was spending the night. He excitedly explained the general's terms, saying that at least now the couple had a chance.

"A chance indeed!" sighed Reb Levi Yitzchok. "Perhaps one chance in a million. Why, we could never raise half that sum in a month, let alone one afternoon!"

Reb Mendel finally persuaded Reb Levi Yitzchok that if they did not start, they would surely never succeed. They decided to ask Reb Shneur Zalman, a younger though equally great *tzaddik,* to accompany them. Reb Shneur Zalman eagerly agreed, but only on one condition — that they would follow his opinion completely on every phase of this mission. His first condition was that they draw up a list of all the townspeople.

"But we know everyone here," they argued. "Besides, it would waste precious time. Remember we have only until tonight."

But Reb Shneur Zalman insisted, and they quickly drew up the list. When they finished, Reb Shneur Zalman told them to check if they had forgotten anyone.

After a minute's silence, Reb Levi Yitzchok said, "Well, there's Velvel, the wealthy miser. He wouldn't even give you a penny for the long climb up the hill to his secluded house. If you insist, we'll put him at the bottom of the list."

"No, he shall be our first stop. Remember our conditions. You must do what I say or I don't go with you."

So they started the long walk to the mansion of Velvel the Miser, knowing in their hearts that nothing would come of their trouble.

They reached his massive home and were shown to his library. Velvel sat and listened with interest to the pitiful story they unfolded, and tears crept into his eyes. But when he got up and opened his safe and beheld all his riches, a hard look spread over his features. His hand reached past the gold and silver coins, past all the precious gems, and from a dusty corner he took one single penny — green with age. He offered it to Reb Mendel, who merely stared at the green coin, dumbfounded. Reb Shneur Zalman quickly took it, saying, "*Tizkeh lemitzvos harbei* — Thank you kindly; may you be worthy of fulfilling many more *mitzvos*."

They left quickly and silently. What good was one rusty penny, when they needed five thousand rubles? Why, that heartless skinflint deserves to have it thrown back in his face, thought Reb Mendel and Reb Levi Yitzchok, angry and disappointed. They had reached the huge stone wall that surrounded the house when a voice called them back. It was Velvel, running after them.

"Forgive me, forgive me for giving you so little. Please come back with me!" he pleaded.

He led them back to his library and went to his safe and took out a handful of coins — not gold or silver coins, but copper pennies! Together they may have added up to three or four rubles.

Reb Shneur Zalman quickly took the money and thanked him in the same manner, while the others turned away even more disappointed than before. Again they left the house and again they were called back This time Velvel offered them silver coins among the pennies ... Again they left, and again they were called back. Ten times this was repeated, each time with **more silver** until Velvel began adding gold pieces. Finally, he gave them **the complete five thousand rubles!**

❧ ❧ ❧

It was half an hour later and the three rabbis were joyfully returning to the village with the ransomed orphan boy. Suddenly, from behind they heard a roar of horse hooves and a wildly careening carriage coming at them at a terrific speed. Had the drunken general changed his mind? They had no time to think. The four men ducked into the bushes along the roadside. They waited while the carriage rushed past them and crashed against the railing of the nearby bridge, tumbling into the water. Cautiously they approached the rushing waters and peered at the churning wreck below.

As the stunned group silently walked away, the orphan stumbled against a heavy chest and quickly called the others to him. Opening it, they discovered the whole five thousand rubles, besides precious jewels and coins!

"This is truly a miracle!" cried Reb Mendel. "Hashem watches over his children. See, he has even sent a royal wedding present to this fatherless boy."

The wedding was truly a royal one. All the townspeople attended, in their Shabbos best. Their singing and dancing lasted until morning without stop, until it was time for the morning prayers.

After the prayers Reb Shneur Zalman approached Reb Mendel and Reb Levi Yitzchok, because he felt he owed them an explanation.

"A desperately poor man," he told them, "once came to Velvel on a cold winter evening to ask for a donation for his daughter's wedding needs. Velvel offered him a penny — only to have it thrown back at him. Being a miser, Velvel decided that from then on he would offer that same penny to every beggar, until someone would appreciate the value of that penny as much as he did. Each time someone came to him for a contribution, the same penny was offered. It was always refused and again put back into the same dusty corner of his safe. Layers of tarnish grew around the penny, and layers of hardness grew around Velvel's heart.

"I knew that Velvel was our only hope for the sum we needed," continued Reb Shneur Zalman. "When I accepted the rusty penny, I penetrated the outer crusts surrounding his heart and he was able to feel pity again. Ten times we had to come back until we were finally successful in scraping off the tarnish from Velvel's heart."

Kindness Repaid

A true story, only the names have been changed
by Rochel Feder

He sat there alone in the back of the shul, watching the men put on their coats. His name was Shimon Shuster, and he was a short, frail-looking man in his late fifties. His face was grayish, almost white in color, and if you looked at his eyes carefully, you could see the frantic look of a man who had not had a decent meal in a long time.

Ever since his family died at the hands of the Nazis, his life had been a hard one — full of loneliness and poverty; but now, on this Friday night, he was more miserable than ever before. He had always tried to support himself — no matter how hard or humiliating the job was. He would go from shul to shul, offering to sweep and wash the floors. He would deliver packages for the fish market on Thursdays. And sometimes on Fridays, the fruit store would also have some deliveries for him. He was happy and grateful for whatever tips people gave him, but sometimes he would carry a heavy order for many blocks, through the snow or pouring rain, and when he finally reached the house, nobody would answer the bell, and he would get no tip at all. With the money that he earned he would pay the rent for his little room, but then there was little left for food, and often he would wish for a plate of hot soup on a cold winter night. His room was in a damp cellar without heat, and he would frequently catch colds. Then he would lie in bed, alone and miserable, unable to work. And yet, he never complained to anybody. He never wanted to bother people with his troubles. His cellar was very chilly, but at least he had a bed, and that was certainly better than sleeping on a hard bench in a park or a shul, as he had years before.

Yet being poor did not bother him as much as being lonely. It was so hard to be without a family, to be without people who really cared. But Shimon had a good way of fighting his loneliness. He would go to hospitals to visit sick people and try to make things easier for them. He spent his time trying to help others who were perhaps less fortunate than he, and this gave him great satisfaction.

The nights were hardest. Sometimes he was tired enough to fall asleep immediately, but there were other times when he would lie in bed, tossing and turning, remembering his family, his sweet innocent children, taken from him so cruelly by those Nazi beasts — and it would be hours before he would finally fall asleep, his pillow wet with tears.

❉ ❉ ❉

Now he sat in the back of the shul, watching the fathers help their children put on their boots. It was a cold, snowy night, and he was very hungry. He had become very weak during the past weeks and that morning when he tried to get off the bed, everything went black and he fainted. A neighbor found him and called a doctor. That was when he got the news.

"Mr. Shuster, you are a very sick man," the doctor said. "You are suffering from malnutrition and if you don't find a way to eat better, you won't hold out much longer."

Now he knew that if he wanted to be well he would have to do what he had always hoped he would never have to do. Once, years before, he had heard about a man named Yankel Fried — a man whose doors were always open to the poor or lonely. Shimon knew where he lived. He often passed his house, but never did he go in. Tonight he would. He had no choice. He had no food and no money. He had been sick with a bad cold for two weeks and he had not earned a penny during that time.

He put on his coat and walked out of shul. It was a light coat and he shivered in the cold. His heart was very heavy as he thought of knocking on the door and asking for a meal. He was almost there when he panicked and thought of turning back, but he made himself go on. He came to the door and softly, very hesitantly, knocked. In a moment the door opened and a tall man, Mr. Fried, stood there. "I ... wh ... I" — Shimon could not speak. He did not know what to say.

"*Gut Shabbos, Reb Yid.* Come in. It's freezing outside!" Mr. Fried greeted him as if he had expected him.

He helped him take off his coat and led him into the dining room, cheerfully announcing, "Rivka! *Kinderlach!* We have a guest!"

Then, turning to Shimon he asked, "And what is your name, sir?"

"Um … my name is Shimon, Shuster. I really don't know how to thank … "

"Oh, but there's nothing to thank. We love to have guests for *Shabbos!*"

At once the four little Fried children were all around him. "Shimon, sit near me! Please, Shimon!" they pleaded.

Shimon looked around him — at the long table with the snowy white cloth, the shining candlesticks, the *challos* covered with a beautiful blue cover. He looked at the sweet, friendly children and at the other poor people — people like him — who sat at the table, and his heart was filled with a happiness that he had not known in years. His voice trembled with emotion as he said the *Kiddush. Oh, how wonderful … to spend a Shabbos* with other Jews … not alone in a cold room! The *challos* were home-made and delicious — just like his wife used to make. Then came gefilte fish, followed by the golden chicken soup with fluffy *kneidlach* floating inside. Everything was so good. And the Frieds wanted so much for him to be satisfied.

"Have another piece of chicken," Mrs. Fried urged. "*Est gezunterheit* (eat in good health) — we have plenty more."

During the meal they sang *zemiros* (Shabbos songs). The children joined in, and Shimon sat there, feeling like one of the family.

It was late. The candles had burned out and everybody was tired. The other guests left to go home, but Mrs. Fried insisted that Shimon sleep at their home, and not go home to his cold cellar room. The guest room was a simple little room, but the bed was comfortable and the quilt was nice and warm. He put his head down on the soft white pillow and felt happy and content. Suddenly there was a knock on the door.

"Yes?" he called.

Eight-year-old Moshe appeared in his pajamas. "Would you like another pillow, Shimon? Some people like two pillows. Here, take mine."

"Oh no, Moshe. It's fine just as it is. Thanks, anyway."

"Here, Shimon," the boy insisted. "I don't need it. Here."

Moshe gave him the pillow, said "*Gut Shabbos,*" and left the room. Shimon put his head down on the pillows, pulled the cover up to his chin, and promptly fell asleep.

❀ ❀ ❀

That was the first *Shabbos* that Shimon spent at the Frieds'. Afterwards, they insisted that he come for every *Shabbos* and *Yom Tov*, and whenever he wanted to during the week. Sometimes, Mr. Fried would give him a few dollars and that was a big help. They were not rich people, but they lived very simply so they would have money to give others. Mrs. Fried's white *Shabbos* apron was worn, and there were no expensive drapes or carpets in the house. Everything was plain, but there was always plenty of good food. When he was depressed, Shimon would talk to Mr. Fried, and Mr. Fried would tell him, "Don't worry, Shimon. *Hashem* loves you dearly because you try so hard to be a good Jew. When *Mashiach* comes, you'll have the greatest reward and the greatest honors, for *Hashem* loves all His children and especially people like you."

❀ ❀ ❀

It was on a *Chanukah*, two years after Shimon started coming to the Fried's, that the fire broke out. They were all playing *dreidel* in the kitchen, except for three-year-old Sarah, who was asleep in her bed, when they heard the screams — horrible, blood-curdling screams. Sarah — little Sarah — was screaming, "Fire!" They all rushed towards the dining room where the candles had been lit, but smoke and flames blocked their way and they could not go in.

Mrs. Fried was yelling frantically. "Sarah! Sarah!" and the children were holding on to her and crying and screaming hysterically, while Mr. Fried and Shimon tried desperately to get the child. The smoke was blinding and they were all choking and coughing. Mr. Fried collapsed on the floor but Shimon — poor, skinny, old Shimon — did not panic. While the neighbors helped Mrs. Fried with the children, Shimon quickly dragged his good friend out of the house. Then, back into the smoke and flames he ran, desperately trying to find they little girl. The heat was unbearable. He knew he would not hold out much longer, but he had to find Sarah.

"Please, *Hashem,* please help me," he pleaded. "They've been so good to me."

He felt as if his heart would burst as he groped about in the thick, black smoke. And then he found her … then he saw the little blonde head under the bed. With his last measure of strength he dragged her to a window and somehow he threw himself out, with the child, unconscious, in his arms.

❀ ❀ ❀

When he opened his eyes, a nurse was standing at his bedside and he gradually realized that he was in a hospital. "Sarah," he moaned. "Where is Sarah?"

"The little girl is doing beautifully, sir, thanks to you. You are a brave man."

"You mean — you mean, she's alive?"

"Yes, sir. She'll be going home soon. Now you just rest and don't worry. Everything's going to be fine. I'm going to tell the Frieds that you're all right. They've been taking turns sleeping in the waiting room until you got better."

He lay there quietly, looking out the window near his bed. It was a beautiful night. The moon was silvery and the stars sparkled like so many diamonds against the deep blue velvety heaven. Shimon was tired, but oh, so happy, too. "Thank You, *Hashem*," he whispered, his heart bursting with gratitude. "Thank You so much for letting me repay my friends."

The Greatest Gift of All

by Leah Herskowitz

It was the first day after *Succos* and Laya was excited to be going back to school. There was Brachah, her best friend, waiting for her. Laya ran to her, school-bag flying.

"Hi!"

"It's about time, slow-poke! How's everything? Did you have a nice *Yom Tov*? Did Blima start to walk yet?" The words came tumbling out; Brachah seldom paused for breath or for answers. "Guess what, Laya, we have a new girl from Hungary in our class. She looks so shy and so different."

Laya and Brachah stood a minute in the doorway of the classroom. The girls were gathered in little groups, catching up on news of the holiday. Sonya sat alone, pretending to be absorbed in her new American book. She was thin and pale, and yes, she did look different.

Laya stood still for a moment, thinking. Then, she smiled and ran in. "Hi! I'm Laya, and you must be Sonya Weiss. I must say, Sonya, you're so smart to pick the best seat in the room — right next to me."

Brachah stood open-mouthed. It really wasn't Laya's seat. At least, it *hadn't* been, but it certainly was now. That was how it began. Days

passed into weeks, and Laya and Sonya, from two different worlds, came to love each other. Still, a barrier remained between them. Laya often invited Sonya to her home to do homework, but Sonya always refused, so they had to stay in class late to study together. Sonya spoke often about her parents, her brothers and sisters, but never invited Laya to her home.

Winter was on its way; a light snow had fallen, but Sonya was still wearing the same gray jacket she wore when she first came to class. It must have been made from some marvelous European cloth because, as Sonya smilingly explained to Laya, "It's really wonderful! When the weather is cold, it makes me feel so warm."

At last Laya knew that Sonya would *have* to come to her house. Laya's mother had told her she could have a birthday party in honor of her twelfth birthday, the day when she would become responsible to keep all the *mitzvos* of a Jewish woman. It would be on a *Shabbos* afternoon, and she could invite her whole class.

Laya hugged her mother with joy. "Oh thanks, Mommy. Now you'll be able to meet Sonya, and maybe you'll be able to make her smile and be happy. I try so much and she tries too, but there's something bothering her. I wish I knew how to help her."

Laya stayed up late, making fancy invitations to give to her classmates. Next morning there were cries of Oh! and Ah! as the girls admired the pretty folded squares. Only Sonya looked at hers without comment.

"Don't you like it, Sonya? Aren't you happy I'm inviting you to my party?"

Sonya forced a smile. "Oh yes, it's lovely, but I — I don't think I'll be able to come."

"Of course you'll come! It's about time you came over on *Shabbos*. You'll have fun, I promise you."

Sonya stood gazing into space and shook her head. Laya was puzzled; not only puzzled, but hurt and annoyed. Angry thoughts went through her mind. "Here I tried so hard to help Sonya and to make her feel at home. Why can't she act like the other girls? Why can't she ever come on *Shabbos* to visit me? Why doesn't she ever invite me to her house? Well, I've tried hard enough, I'm mad!" And Laya went and took her books from her desk and sat down in a back seat.

That day both girls were miserable. Laya thought about Sonya all day, one minute hating her for her coldness and the next minute thinking, "What's the trouble? Why is she like this? What can I do to help her?"

When class was dismissed, Sonya slowly gathered her books, put on her "wondrous, warm jacket" and walked sadly, thoughtfully homeward. She did not realize she was being followed by Laya. They walked through a run-down neighborhood Laya had never seen before. How many blocks was it now, ten, twenty? No wonder Sonya had usually stayed home on bad rainy days. Finally, on a narrow, shabby street, Sonya stopped at the side of a shoe repair shop, opened the door, and walked in.

Laya pictured Sonya walking up narrow, dingy flights of stairs and from the love and compassion in her heart, she suddenly understood. "That's why she hardly ever smiles! Why was I so blind? All I could think about was my party and I never realized that poor Sonya is *ashamed* to come because she doesn't even own a *Shabbos* dress. How can I help her?" As soon as Laya got home, she rushed to the phone to consult Brachah. Together they called Miss Weberman, their teacher, who told them she would speak to the principal immediately.

Rabbi Goldfischer was the smartest, kindest principal in the whole world — and the fastest-working, also. He stopped off at the Weiss home that very evening to "welcome Mr. and Mrs. Weiss to the community." He told them what an outstanding student Sonya was and what fine work she was doing. Mrs. Weiss went to the kitchen to make tea and the two men sat and talked about the years in Hungary. With tears in his eyes, Mr. Weiss told of secret sacrifices they made every day in their struggle to remain true to *Torah*. Rabbi Goldfischer was filled with admiration for the bravery of these quiet, modest people. As he listened and looked around at the poorly furnished apartment, he felt grateful to Laya for giving him this opportunity to help. No one deserved it more than the Weiss family.

"Have you heard about our "Welcome Stranger Loan Fund"?", the Rabbi asked.

Mr. and Mrs. Weiss had not; in fact, no one else had ever heard of it either. Rabbi Goldfischer explained that the school had a special fund which could be used for only one purpose, to provide loans for the families of new students. Every family moving into a new neighborhood runs into big expenses, and the "Welcome Stranger Loan Fund" was the school's way of letting newcomers know that they were among good friends and neighbors, who were anxious to make them feel at home. The loan could be repaid whenever it was convenient — in a few weeks, a few months, even a few years. Mr. and

Mrs. Weiss would not accept charity, but, as Rabbi Goldfischer explained the fund, it was a *loan* — who could refuse?

Mission accomplished, the Rabbi called Miss Weberman who called the anxiously awaiting Laya with the good news. Laya and Brachah got busy on the phone mapping out a secret *tzedakah* campaign to raise money quickly and quietly. Without mentioning names, they explained to their friends and their parents' friends that this was for a needy, deserving family.

How kind people were, how understanding! They all realized that there was no need to inquire into the personal details, so as not to risk embarrassing people who were suffering enough already. The sincerity of Laya and Brachah were enough for them.

Generous as ever, Aunt Dora said, "Sure, darling, I've been saving some money on clothes lately by sewing my own. Now I know why I did it. I'll mail you a check tonight."

Judy, Laya's older sister who was now a "working girl," promised to contribute her "*maaser* money" (a tenth of her earnings set aside for *tzedakah)* for the next three weeks, and to ask her friends to do likewise.

Brachah's Uncle Joe believed in quick action. Within fifteen minutes after he received the phone call, he knocked at Brachah's door with his contribution. "And listen honey, maybe the man wants a job in my bakery? Or maybe I can help find him a job someplace else? That's the type of help they might appreciate more than money."

When an exhausted Laya said the *Shema* that night before going to sleep, she said a special prayer to Hashem for things to go so smoothly and for her to be able to help the Weiss family without hurting their feelings.

Next morning, Laya went to school and went back to her old seat next to Sonya. She was rewarded by seeing a slow smile turn up the corner of Sonya's mouth. Sonya reached over shyly and took Laya's hand. "Guess what, Laya, I can come to your party!"

It was *Erev Shabbos,* busy as usual, and even a little more so because of preparations for the party. Everyone pitched in, and even Brachah came over to help make potato salad and spring salad.

Mother called, "Will someone go to the door? Someone's knocking, but you're so busy talking you don't hear."

There was Sonya and her father holding a big, beautiful cake, decorated with rosettes and flowers, tempting and luscious. Brachah and Laya gaped, their eyes wide with admiration and their mouths watering. "Just a little present for your birthday," said Mr. Weiss. "You know I used to be baker in Europe and — "

"Baker," screamed Brachah, "What a coincidence! My uncle Joe is looking for a baker to work in his bakery."

Now it was Mr. Weiss's turn to get excited. "Do you mean it? Really? Perhaps I can get a job!"

Brachah and Laya had already run to the phone to call Uncle Joe. Back they ran and thrust a slip of paper with the address into the hands of a man trembling with joy. After a noisy exchange of thanks, Mr. Weiss left, walking a little straighter already, and Sonya stayed awhile to help.

Laya slipped away from her chattering friends. She walked slowly and pensively to her room, closed the door and lay down in her bed to cry tears of joy. How happy she was, how lucky she was, to be able to celebrate her twelfth birthday with a *mitzvah* of *tzedakah*. *Hashem* had given her the greatest gift of all, the gift of being able to help someone else.

Escape ... Impossible!

A true story, only the names have been changed
by Ursula Lehmann

It was our people's darkest hour. First, for weeks, new people had been brought to the gates each day. From city and town, from hiding places in homes and in the woods, the Nazis rounded up all the Jewish people and squeezed them into the ghetto.

There was illness. There was hunger. There was cold and not enough clothing. There was no milk. Aaron was hungry too. His father, the famous Rabbi Radinski, could get no extra food. The little the Nazis permitted, the Rabbi often gave away to sick people or to babies. Aaron tried not to complain, but it was not easy. Times had been bad, but now they were getting even worse. The deportations started. Each day, names were put on a list, and each day, as the men and women and children whose names were on the list were rounded up, the terror grew. Perhaps tomorrow my name will be on the list? Perhaps tomorrow the Gestapo will push me at gunpoint onto the cattle-car of a train and send me to a death camp? Rabbi Radinski had managed to get foreign papers for his wife and daughters. There was hope their lives would be saved — if only the Nazis accepted the visa and travel permit. But for himself and Aaron, who had no papers, escape was ... impossible.

Then came that fateful day. A friend slipped to the corner of the room that Rabbi Radinski and his son occupied, and warned them,

"Your names are on the lists for tomorrow. I saw them. It is no use any longer to hope some foreign papers will come for you. After tomorrow it will be too late."

Aaron shivered. He had heard every word. He looked at his father's face — though it was thinned by hunger and despair for his people, it was calm — and Aaron became less afraid. He saw his father was whispering a silent prayer to *Hashem*, so he too began to *daven*. G-d would hear.

There was no time to lose. Now was the time for "certain previously made plans" to be used. Through a secret passageway, Rabbi Radinski and his son escaped from the heavily guarded ghetto, and they made their way to the railroad station.

Once there, Aaron could not help but be afraid. All around them were German soldiers and there they sat, he and his father, wearing their normal Jewish ghetto clothes. Rabbi Radinski wore his usual black hat on his head. His flowing beard and *payos* covered part of his hunger-thinned face, and his long black jacket was his only protection against the wind. He and Aaron, who was dressed the same way, were obviously Jews, and any passerby could see it. Rabbi Radinski had refused to wear a disguise.

Suddenly Aaron heard his father's voice speaking quietly, though his face was turned straight ahead. No one could see that Rabbi Radinski was speaking to his son, but Aaron listened.

"My son," he said, "you must do something very difficult now. Do not think of the soldiers — not even for a moment! Do not look at the people. Do not even look at the scenery around you. Look only inside yourself, to your mind and heart, and think. Think of *Hashem* and His greatness. Concentrate on Him. It has been said in the *Nefesh Ha-chayim* of Rav Chaim of Volozhin," Rabbi Radinski continued gravely, "that anyone who concentrates with all his might on a certain *possuk* will not be harmed. The *possuk* is: אַתָּה הָרְאֵתָ לָדַעַת כִּי ה' הוּא הָאֱלֹקִים אֵין עוֹד מִלְבַדּוֹ, *You have been shown to know that Hashem is the L-rd; there is nothing else but Him.'*

"Now let this *possuk* fill your mind. Think of nothing else. Think only that *Hashem* is everywhere. Throughout our trip, concentrate with the knowledge that there is nothing else; only *HaKodosh Baruch Hu* (G-d). It is our only defense. He is our hope."

Aaron thought his father was asking him to do the impossible, but when he saw his father's bravery, he knew he had to try. It was difficult. It was *very* difficult not to think of those hated uniforms that marched to and fro throughout the station. It was hard not to wonder where they were going and what would be their fate. But Aaron remembered his father's words and he tried.

"אַתָּה הָרְאֵתָ לָדַעַת ..." Now they were on the train. The wheels were turning ... "אֵין עוֹד מִלְּבַדּוֹ". The train stopped and started again ... more people got on ... There is none else but Him ... some got off ... *Hashem* is the L-rd ... soldiers boarded, laughing and joking, Nazi soldiers! ... There is none but Him ... Aaron and his father in their Jewish ghetto clothes, concentrated with all their might ... *There is none beside Hashem* ... The train slowed to a stop.

"*Raus, raus,*" shouted the soldiers. "Everyone out."

Aaron and his father joined the others as they slowly filed out of the train, to stand on the snow-covered grass next to the tracks. As Aaron looked around with growing horror, the Nazi soldiers began examining each passenger's identity papers. Catastrophe had come!

Now the soldiers had only three people more to examine before reaching Rabbi Radinski. Quietly the Rabbi turned to Aaron. "You are not concentrating!" he said.

It was true. In his excitement and fear Aaron had forgotten.

"אַתָּה הָרְאֵתָ לָדַעַת ..." he began again, with all his might.

The nearest soldier suddenly stopped in the midst of examining a passport. "All aboard," he called. "Everyone back on."

The frightened people looked up with relieved surprise and boarded again. The train rolled on, with Rabbi Radinski and Aaron aboard, deep in all-encompassing thought.

The train traveled all the way across Poland to the Russian border without being disturbed again. Aaron hardly noticed. He was concentrating.

At the border, the passengers stepped down from the train and lined up to file across. It was already early morning. The border gates were only kept open at certain times; they might close any moment.

"Wait," said Rabbi Radinski. "It is time to *daven Shacharis.* The border will wait."

Though others urged them to cross, Rabbi Radinski did not listen. It was time for *Shacharis.* He and Aaron *davened,* and the gates swung closed.

When they finished, the border guards opened the gates again without a word, and quietly let the two Jews, father and son, pass through to safety.

❀ ❀ ❀

Today, "Aaron" (as we called him) is a grown man living in *Eretz Yisrael.* He is a famous Torah scholar who leads a great yeshivah, and his learning helps keep the light of Torah bright among our people. By his real name he is known to many of you, and surely to your parents.

So did *Hashem* work one more of His many miracles in those tragic times.

The Most Beautiful Home in Israel

by Rochel Feder

Nine-year old Moshe stood on the deck of the ship, looking out over the gently rippling waters. "Soon our dream will come true and we'll be in *Eretz Yisrael*. How good it will be to live as Jews and not be afraid."

It was 1965. Moshe Baum and his family were among the few fortunate people who were able to leave Russia and come to Israel.

Moshe thought of the beautiful home that they had left behind, and of his father's farm. They had not been allowed to take anything along and they had very little money with them. "Probably Tatty (father) will be a farmer here, too," he thought, "for that's what he's always done and that's what he knows best."

And then he remembered ... "It's the *Shemittah* year (the seventh year, when it is forbidden to plant in *Eretz Yisrael)*!" Only a short time ago he and his friends, Yidel and Hillel, had been sitting with their *rebbi* in Hillel's cold cellar and the *rebbi*, Reb Mottele, had told them about the *Shemittah* year, when Jews in *Eretz Yisrael* must not work their farms and orchards.

"I guess Tatty will have to look for some other type of work. But, oh how wonderful, to be in *Eretz Yisrael* among Jews who know about *Shemittah* and keep all the laws. Now I won't have to hide in a cellar when I learn with my *rebbi*, and tremble with fear every time the doorbell rings. Oh, *Hashem*, how good you are to us! If only our friends in Russia could also be so lucky!"

Their hearts bursting with happiness, Moshe's father and mother, Jacob and Rivka, and their six children left the ship. Hot tears ran down their cheeks as they pressed their lips to the beloved earth and kissed it again and again. "*Boruch Hashem*," they kept on saying, 'We are here at last!"

For the first few days the Baums stayed with friends and afterwards they moved into a small, one-room apartment. Jobs were very scarce in Israel and Jacob was forced to accept odd jobs with long hours and little pay. Jacob planned to find work on a farm — the work he knew and loved — as soon as the *Shemittah* year was over.

So the Baums settled down. They knew that they had very little, yet they also knew that they had very much. Their clothes were old and worn hand-me-downs from people who didn't need them anymore, and their furniture was second-hand. But if somebody would have asked them, "Would you like to go back to your big beautiful house in Russia?", they would have said, "No, no, no! A thousand times no! It's true we have no money now, but we are in *Eretz Yisrael*, we are free, we can live as Jews and not be afraid."

Once a week, the Baums felt wealthy — that was *Shabbos*. Every Friday Rivka cooked fish and chicken and all kinds of other good things

Lekavod Shabbos (in honor of *Shabbos*). Every Friday she baked golden-brown *challos* and she even let the children help braid their own small *challos* before she put them in the oven. Their house smelled wonderful from all the cooking and baking and the whole family was happy because *Shabbos* was coming. Nobody noticed that the tablecloth was worn; nobody noticed that the flowers were in a simple jar instead of a fancy crystal vase. To Jacob and his family the table looked lovely. As they sat there, singing *zemiros* (*Shabbos* songs) and eating the good foods that had been prepared with so much love, they felt richer than the richest king.

It was on a Friday night, about six months after their arrival, that old Tanta Bayla came to visit. The girls had finished clearing off the table and everybody was sitting quietly, listening eagerly to their father, who was telling the story of the *Sidrah* (weekly Torah portion).

"My rheumatism has been bothering me a lot lately, and I don't go out much, but I just had to come and see how you are," Tante Bayla said.

Slowly she sipped hot tea and looked around the room. She saw the worn old tablecloth, the plain jar with flowers, saw all of the shabbiness in that simple little room. "You poor dears," she murmured, pressing Rivka's hand, "you came all the way from Russia, and now this is all you have ... this plain little room ...? You can barely move around in here. Why, how do you manage?"

"It's not bad," Rivka quietly replied.

"Not bad?" cried the old woman. "Why, it's terrible! To live like this!" There was an embarrassed silence.

"Jacob!" Tanta Bayla's voice was suddenly cold and harsh. "How can you do this to Rivka? Look at her! Look at the children! Borrow money and buy yourself a farm! Don't you care about your family? What kind of a man are you, anyway?"

It hurt the little ones to hear somebody speak to their father like that. Somehow they didn't like Tanta Bayla so much any more.

But Jacob Baum was patient as always, and he said, "We know you mean well, Tanta Bayla, but this is the *Shemittah* year and we are forbidden to work the fields."

For a moment it was very quiet in the room, and then … "Look," Tanta Bayla went on, and her voice was softer now, "believe me, I love you all and that's why I'm talking this way. If I didn't care, I wouldn't say anything."

Then Rivka turned to their aunt and said, "Dear Tanta Bayla, there are many laws in our Torah that are hard for us to understand, but one thing we must always remember. *Hashem* is our Father, and we are His children. He loves us dearly, as all fathers love their children, and wants only the best for us. Every seventh year we must let our fields rest, just as every *Shabbos* we must rest. It is true that this is a difficult time for us, but we believe, as Jews must always believe, that *Hashem* will help us. Don't worry," she added softly, "we'll be fine."

"Oh, Rivka, you're a good girl and you make very nice speeches, but you just don't know how it *hurts* me to see you living in this *dump* here!"

Tanta Bayla was not yet finished. "Every time I see you in that shabby coat of yours … I just feel *terrible*. Why should you live this way?"

Once again Rivka spoke and her voice was calm and gentle. "Maybe you just don't understand what it means to me … to be here in *Eretz Yisrael* … to be able to keep the *mitzvah* of *Shemittah*."

Slowly she began … "Back in Russia I used to sit home at night and wonder and worry why Jacob was not home yet. I would try to keep busy … with a little sewing or reading … but always I was worrying … Maybe they've found out … found out about the little hiding place that's our *shul* … found out that he wears a *yarmulke* and *tzitzis* and puts on *tefillin* every day … Maybe they've arrested him … Maybe he'll never come home again …" Her face was clouded with sadness now. "It happened to others, Tanta Bayla. Many Jews were taken away and never came home again."

The children listened quietly. They remembered those nights,

nights when she seemed restless, worried ... but they had never known why. Now they understood.

"I would go to a friend ... to visit ... and I would wonder, maybe there's a tape recorder someplace, taping my words ... Maybe she's *not* really a friend ... maybe they've told her to watch us ... to spy on us ... How do I know that I can trust her? Who ... whom can I trust? Is there anybody at all?

"I had a beautiful house, Tanta Bayla," she went on, "and nice clothes ... but I was not happy. I was ready to give away everything ... to have this ... this life that I have now!

"Now my children can go to a *yeshivah* and not hide in a cold cellar. Now I can enjoy hearing the way they study their *Chumash*, loud and clear ... and unafraid. This is my life," she whispered, and her soft brown eyes were shining with tears. "*This* is my pleasure ... *not* a beautiful coat.

"We thought we were doomed ... we thought it was hopeless ... We'd *never* go out ... And *Hashem* had mercy on us and heard our prayers and that miracle happened ... Can you imagine our joy when we found out that we were coming here ? No, I don't think you can. I don't think that anybody who hasn't been there can possibly imagine that kind of happiness ...

"How do you think I should show my gratitude to *Hashem?* By

telling my husband to work the fields and tend the crops during the *Shemittah* year? For a coat?

"No, Tanta Bayla. For the coat will fade ... but the *mitzvah* of *Shemittah* will never fade. This *mitzvah* will be very precious to *Hashem* ... because even though it's hard on us now, we perform it with joy anyway."

"Moshele," Rivka said, turning to her eldest son, "tell Tanta Bayla what Reb Mottele taught you about *Shemittah.*"

Loud and clear, Moshe repeated the words that his *rebbi* in Russia had spoken ... in a cold cellar ... not so very long ago ...

"Those who will keep the laws of *Shemittah* will be blessed. The earth will give her fruits and Jews will have plenty to eat and they will sit in the land, secure in the knowledge that they will not be driven out of *Eretz Yisrael.* And if Jews wonder what will we eat in the seventh year, then *Hashem* promises us that enough will grow in the sixth year to last until the next crop is harvested."

Old Tanta Bayla sat there, deep in thought. Finally she lifted her head, and cleared her throat. She was smiling now, and her voice was gentle and warm. "I like your room. It's a beautiful room. I haven't seen such a beautiful room in a long time."

The Locket of Hope

A true story by Rena (Brown) Kaplan

I slumped onto a large rock and trembled in the warm, sunny schoolyard. I gulped nervously as my hand reached up to feel beneath the neckline of my dress for the missing locket. Again, a stab of anguish and fear. The locket was gone!

My eyes darted frantically over the sandy ground searching desperately. Panicky thoughts raced wildly through my mind. Were discovery and death to be the end of my lost secret? My confused thoughts traveled back to the morning two years before when the locket had first begun to dominate my thoughts.

❧ ❧ ❧

I had been finishing breakfast together with my younger brothers and sisters. The atmosphere was tense as it had been every day for several weeks, that tragic winter of 1942. Ever since the Germans had occupied the neighboring cities and sent the Jews to concentration camps, everyone realized that it was only a matter of days before Zavichost, too, would be occupied.

The room was unhappily quiet. We had learned to keep our noisy play to our upstairs bedroom.

"Golda," called Mama with forced enthusiasm. "Please come out to the porch. There's something I'd like to discuss with you."

Mama and I sat down on the rocker, our favorite place for intimate conversation. Mama was calm for the first time in weeks, but stubbornly determined. My feet nervously set the rocker in motion as I heard Mama's decisive words in disbelief.

The Stepolskas had offered to adopt one of us. They were Polish Catholics; they had nothing to fear from the Germans, so they would be able to provide a safe home for a Jewish child. The Gestapo was only miles away and chances of survival for a Jew were bleak. This offer was a last chance for life.

Mama explained that I was the best choice for adoption, for two reasons: I was blonde and less Jewish-looking than the other children and, because I was the oldest and very bright, I could use my wits to survive the dangerous years ahead.

The Stepolskas had agreed to adopt me on one major condition; I must embrace their Catholic religion. They would be risking their lives by harboring a Jewish child at a time when all Jews were being hunted down and sent away to die. If they were to say that I was their own child, they demanded that I accept their total life style.

That was why I had to be very strong, Mama said. While I should outwardly show the Stepolskas that I was giving up my Jewish religion, inside I must remain as strong a Jew as ever. My Jewish upbringing would now be put to a terrible test. I must hope for the day when I would be able to live as a Jew again.

My heartbroken Mama urged me to cooperate. My survival would give her strength to cope with the awful misery that was as near as the arrival of the Germans.

Mama's hand darted into her apron pocket and emerged with a small object.

"Your *siddur,* your *Chumash,* must be left behind. This is all you can risk taking."

My cold fingers took the small silver locket, but I was too numb with shock to spring open the clasp. Mama pressed open the spring for me and unrolled the small piece of paper that lay within. Staring up at me, in tiny but clear print were the words שְׁמַע יִשְׂרָאֵל ה' אֱלֹקֵינוּ ה' אֶחָד that were to become the source of all my strength for the years to come.

Quickly, Mama and I packed some things, and, with tears, hugs, promises, and prayers, I left for Breslau to begin a new life with the Stepolskas as their only daughter, "Zasia."

The following week I was in constant fear of being identified as a Jew. I had become so accustomed to a strict curfew and places where a Jew was not allowed to walk, that the sudden thrust of freedom was overwhelming. Every time someone looked at me, I was sure I was being recognized as a Jew.

"How," I wondered anxiously, "would I be able to act like a Catholic, when every instinct within me screamed out against this alien faith?"

The Stepolskas were both professionals: He was a doctor and she was a dentist. They were cultured people and enjoyed the arts. They introduced me to the opera and ballet. Yet, despite the Stepolskas' concern and efforts to make me forget my family, I fell into a terrible sadness. My days were long and dreary. My nights were disturbed by nightmares when I would awaken heartsick, calling for my family and my old way of life.

Shabbos was unbearable. The lights from the huge chandelier seemed dull compared to Mama's dancing candles that used to light up both room and soul. Gossip and politics were a dull substitute for Tatte's (Father's) *divrei Torah.* My only comfort came from the hidden *Sh'ma* in my locket. It seemed to go right through to my heart and make it hurt a little less. My sadness lasted for a long time until one night, I awoke in bed holding my locket, and a flood of determination engulfed me. I made a promise:

''Not only was I going to live through this vicious war — I was going to remain faithful to Hashem!''

I was ready to pretend and go along with this Catholic charade, but I wouldn't let it change me. I, too, was on a battlefield — a spiritual and emotional battlefield. If I couldn't have my family near me, I could at least act in such a way that they would be proud of me. And I would win my own personal war.

Slowly, I repeated the *passuk,* concentrating on every word, שְׁמַע יִשְׂרָאֵל ה' אֱלֹקֵינוּ ה' אֶחָד. *Hashem* had brought me this far; *Hashem* would see me through.

Feeling helpless no longer, I fell into a strength-giving sleep.

The Stepolskas encouraged me to make new friends in school, but I disappointed them. I couldn't bring myself to become close to the Christian girls.

At school I remained a loner. I was always cordial but aloof. Memories took the place of companions. Usually I remained in the classroom during recess, preferring my privacy to the play of classmates. I felt no need to belong. Today, however, I rushed out to the schoolyard, worried about the stares of the schoolmaster; I didn't dare seem to be different than the others.

I wasn't used to joining the crowd in the yard, so I felt uncomfortable. Without thinking, my hand reached up to feel for the locket, my symbol of security. *And that was when I discovered that it had disappeared!*

My mind became a whirlpool of frightening thoughts. If anyone were to discover the locket, spring open the clasp, and recognize the Hebrew letters, an immediate investigation would be made. The backgrounds of all students would be checked. The German agents were efficient and thorough. I could never escape.

Suddenly I tensed. A girl was coming toward me. A thin silver chain was dangling from her hand.

I recognized what she held. My palms became moist. Beads of sweat dotted my forehead.

"I think you lost this," spoke the girl softly. "I opened it."

I swallowed. Neither of us spoke. I closed my eyes and concentrated intently on the words that lay inches away in the silver locket. *"Hashem,"* I implored soundlessly. "Strengthen me!"

Suddenly, from a concealed pocket in the seam of her sleeve, the girl removed a bound piece of cloth. "I saved this when my family left," she said and showed me a piece of parchment from a *mezuzah*.

I stared, slowly understanding that a miracle had happened.

I uttered a hushed "Thank you" to *Hashem* as she handed me the locket.

In eager but cautious whispers we began to talk. Finally, two terribly lonely Jewish girls had each found a friend to give her strength. A friendship began that would keep growing stronger during the four years we would yet endure in Breslau.

※ ※ ※

In 1945, at the close of the war, Golda, as Zasia was now able to call herself, returned to Zavichost in the hope of tracing her family. She approached the Jewish Rescue Committee who smuggled her across the Polish border, and then helped her to establish contact with relatives in America. These relatives paid for her to come to the United States as a student.

Golda remembered the promise she had made as young Zasia in Breslau. Today, about thirty years later, as wife and mother, Golda is proud of her Jewish family. Her children attend yeshivos; her eldest son learns in Israel. On *Shabbos,* illumination has returned to her home. The light of the candles blend with the light of *divrei Torah,* the blessing of a promise fulfilled.

The Phantom Neat-nik

by Leah Herskowitz

"What's going on? Am I a combined detective and housekeeper, or a rabbi? First the mystery in the *beis midrash* (study hall), then a problem in the dormitory, and now to top it off, the Ladies' Auxiliary is coming Sunday afternoon to inspect the dormitory! May Hashem send me the wisdom to cope with it all!"

Yes, Rabbi Bergman, the poor *mashgiach* (dean of the study hall) in the yeshiva, really had troubles. Not that the *beis midrash* mystery was a bad problem. It just bothered him because he did not know who the mysterious benefactor was. It has started the day after *Yom Kippur.* As the boys left the *shul* after *Yom Kippur davening,* Rabbi Bergman looked around at the sad state of the *beis midrash* — chairs and benches upset, *machzorim* and *siddurim* everywhere, and everyone rushing out to eat after the fast. But early the next morning, when the *mashgiach* came in at 5:30 A.M. for his regular study session before the *minyan,* he stood in the doorway and blinked. Was he dreaming, had he sleep-walked, or was the scene before him real? The *beis midrash* was completely transformed. Everything was neatly arranged, clean and orderly. Could this be the same room? It couldn't be, yet it was! **Who did it?** After questioning everyone, it seemed that the secret benefactor was Mr. Nobody — because nobody claimed credit for it, or could contribute any knowledge about it.

The opposite sort of problem existed in the dormitory. The boys were not taking proper care of their rooms or their clothing, and the entire building had a messy air about it. One of the chief culprits was Mordechai, more popular known as Mordy the Mess. Everybody loved Mordy. He was always ready to do anyone a favor, but a model of neatness he was not. Tie askew, shirttails hanging out — if you hadn't seen him polishing his shoes every morning, you would think they hadn't been shined for weeks. Perhaps it was because he was always in a hurry to be first to *minyan,* first in class, first to help out a friend, first to run for any *mitzvah* that he just did not seem to have time to pull himself together.

And his room! It had become a legend in the dormitory. Only Mordy knew how to find the way to his bed through the maze of "important items" that filled his room. Even the cleaning man had long refused to step into it.

Rabbi Bergman had always worried that Mordy's sloppy habits might have a contagious effect on the other boys, and sure enough, a crisis had recently come up. After taking a lot of goodnatured teasing about his room, Mordy had lost his temper, put a lock on the door, and had forbidden anyone to come near it.

And, now! A committee of the Ladies' Auxiliary had decided to inspect the dormitory to see how they could improve it with decorations and other niceties. Rabbi Bergman had heard talk of new shower curtains — good! New light shades in the corridors — fine! But talk of drapes in the students' room? How could he ever explain a room like Mordechai's to these well-meaning ladies? They would probably be outraged and, Heaven forbid, even antagonized. How would he handle this delicate situation?

Rabbi Bergman forced these unpleasant thoughts from his mind, and came back to his first headache. He simply had to solve the *beis midrash* mystery. After the first surprise, the "guilty" party had been continuing his work. Every Friday, early as Rabbi Bergman might come to the *beis midrash,* the Phantom Neat-nik had been there before him, cleaning up after the previous *mishmar* (late study session), making the study hall neat and orderly for *Shabbos.* Well, tonight was Thursday again, and Rabbi Bergman had a plan.

Late that night, after the last *masmidim* (late students) had left the *beis midrash,* Rabbi Bergman dimmed the lights. But instead of leaving, he seated himself in the corner to wait. One o'clock, one thirty, two o'clock. Finally, the *mashgiach* dozed off.

Suddenly he was awakened by footsteps. Aha! The phantom had arrived! Who could this stranger be? The flickering light at the *Aron Kodesh* cast an eerie shadow as the man approached. He walked swiftly to the *Aron Kodesh,* and began fumbling around with something.

"Oh, Oh, What's this?" thought Rabbi Bergman. "I guess this is not our mysterious benefactor. What luck! What a coincidence to be here just in time to catch a thief!"

Rabbi Bergman had heard of young vandals who robbed synagogues — but he certainly was not prepared to catch one here. He

glanced around quickly for a weapon. He seized a chair and, raising it quickly, shouted: "Stop, thief!" The man stood still. The *mashgiach* switched on the light and ran toward the thief.

What? Who? The man of the big shadow had shrunk, and it was only Mordechai — Mordy the Mess — frozen in his tracks, with a feather duster in his hand! Now it was Rabbi Bergman's turn to stand shocked, amazed.

"You! But this is impossible! You cleaning up?" — And the *mashgiach* broke into roars of laughter. He cried from laughter and could not stop. Mordechai stood there getting redder and redder. When the *mashgiach* finally quieted down and put his arm around Mordy, Mordy broke into tears, sobbing.

"I knew people would laugh at me if they heard I had become neat! Just before *Yom Kippur,* our *rebbi* gave us a lecture on the importance of neatness and cleanliness. Since we Jews are Chosen People, we must always be neat and clean, like children of a King. And I decided to change my habits. And it was so hard! That first night after *Yom Kippur*, I was working until four in the morning! And then my room! I worked at it every night till I fixed it up. Do you know why I locked it? So the boys shouldn't laugh at me, like you're laughing at me now!" Mordechai then broke into uncontrollable sobbing.

"Mordy, Mordy, my boy, I'm not laughing at you! Can't you see, I'm laughing from happiness to see how you have raised yourself to such a high level? You are a real *ben Torah* now, Mordy. Now you are a *complete* man. Now you have gained the upper hand over your feelings. Come, let's shake hands on it."

The *mashgiach,* wiping his tears of joy and pride, and Mordy, wiping his own tears on his sleeve, shook hands solemnly and began to set up the *beis midrash* for the next day's sessions.

To The Border

by A. Yussel

The coach of the Grand Duke lay tilted over in a ditch at the side of the road. A work of art, this coach was; fine wood covered with elaborate and delicate carvings, right down to the spokes of the wheels. The Grand Duke's coat of arms stood out brilliantly on the doors. It seemed rather undignified for such a magnificent coach to be sticking up at such a ridiculous angle.

And here was the Grand Duke himself, standing in the middle of the road; a short but enormously fat man with a double chin hanging over a third. On the tip of his first chin was a tiny patch of hair that was supposed to pass for a sporty beard. A bright yellow plume spilled over the brim of his hat, bobbing up and down. He wore a broad leather belt that went around his belly like a hoop around a barrel, and he had a sword and a rich scarlet cape, both dragging at the heels of his boots.

He was saying hotly: "… A wheel came off, eh? … just like that. Well, I swear somebody's going to pay dearly for this!" He coughed. The weather was cold and brisk. "Well, don't stand there, blockheads! I'm freezing!"

The Grand Duke's guards dismounted from their horses, stood around him with their heads bowed in dismay. The Grand Duke pointed at the captain of the guard. "Captain!" he said, "Order your men to search for a vehicle and take anyone that you … wait … what's that I hear?"

There was a low rumbling from far-off down the road. A coach came heaving into sight, traveling at a fast pace. Before long they could clearly see the team of four horses straining in front and the coachman sitting high, bundled in peasant furs, with a bulky cap pulled low over his eyes and a muffler wrapped around the lower part of his face. The captain of the guard quickly mounted his horse and rode to the coach, motioning the driver to stop.

"You will drive His Excellency, the Grand Duke," he commanded curtly, and then returned.

The Grand Duke ordered some of his men to remain with his carriage and prepared to board the other one. A few guards helped him get in, and with considerable effort; the Grand Duke barely fitted through the door, and his weight didn't make it any easier.

The coach was empty. What a contrast to the Grand Duke's own luxurious conveyance! This one was old and battered, needing paint. The upholstery inside was dirty and ragged. A stale odor filled the interior. The Grand Duke winced as he settled back against the hard leather seat. With a jolt and a creak, the coach began moving. Two riders were out in front of them, and the captain of the guard and two others followed in the rear.

The Grand Duke was still shaken up. He had had a close call when his coach careened into the ditch. His driver died with a broken neck. But he knew it was no accident. The front left wheel had been deliberately loosened so it would slide off its axle while in motion. Things like this were happening often lately. There were many who would have been very glad to get rid of the Grand Duke, for he was a tyrant. He was hated by practically everyone in his province, and more so since the trial in Klennitz, two days ago. It was the climax of his wickedness. An innocent man had been sentenced to die — the rabbi of Klennitz.

The rabbi of Klennitz was known throughout the province for his great wisdom and kindness, a *tzaddik* who was fiercely loved by the Jews he led and immensely admired by the gentiles as well. It stung the Grand Duke bitterly to see the rabbi of Klennitz — a Jew — being so unanimously liked, while he, himself, was so popularly detested. His hate for the rabbi grew beyond bounds, until, at last, he firmly resolved to have him killed. But it had to be done "legally," in a manner that would discredit the rabbi in the eyes of the people.

The plan was simple. The Grand Duke let it be known that some secret documents had been stolen. He had faked evidence planted in the rabbi's home. Then came the "trial," with false witnesses and a bribed judge. The rabbi was accused of stealing the documents to sell to a foreign country. He was found guilty as a traitor. His family was sent into exile, at present staying in the village of Zlansdorff, five miles over the border. And next week … the rabbi of Klennitz was going to hang.

The Grand Duke was now on his way back from the trial, returning to his estate. Except for the misfortune of the loose wheel, he was filled with satisfaction. It was a pretty shrewd trick. Yes, sir, he was a genius.

He didn't know it, but there was only one thing wrong with his scheme — the people weren't fooled.

The party reached the Grand Duke's estate. Tall, steel gates swung open and the company turned into the driveway. But now there was somebody else. A lone horseman was following them up the road, riding hard. He turned sharply into the lane, where he was stopped by the two rear guards. A few hurried words, a sharp command, and the horse halted as the rider reined in alongside the coach. He leaned towards the window.

"Your Excellency!" he panted. "The rabbi has escaped!"

"What!"

"He was helped from the outside," the rider continued

breathlessly. "He's going to join his family in Zlansdorff tonight —"

"Captain!" shouted the Grand Duke. "Quick, change the horses! The bridge over the border — it's the only way to get to Zlansdorff. We must get there before he does and cut him off! Aha! I'll trap that scoundrel of a Jew myself!" He coughed.

"Yes, Your Excellency," said the rider, "but he'll most probably be in disguise."

"So what?" said the Grand Duke. "I'll stop every man that tries to cross the bridge." And again he coughed, long and loud.

Soon, the group was back in formation. The guards sat on fresh, eager steeds, and a new team was in harness. The Grand Duke waved his arm from the coach. "To the border!" And the mad ride began.

The procession poured out of the driveway into the road. Trees flashed by as they plunged into the forest; an echoing barrage as they clacked across cobblestones, hurtling through a town, nearly running down some startled pedestrians. Now upward, winding high around a mountainside; now among the open fields. Onward they raced — the guards leaning forward in their saddles, men and horses streaming puffs of white vapor in the cold winter air; the horses foaming, their eyes large and bloodshot, their thudding hooves a deep drumming on the hard-packed ground. The coach rocked and swayed fearfully, creaking and rattling in every joint, the wind whistling by. The Grand Duke hung on tightly to a strap. *That Jew must not get away!* The Grand Duke stuck his head out of the window. His gorgeous hat promptly blew off. "Faster! Faster!" he shouted. A whip cracked, and the coach slowly began overtaking the two guards in front. It passed between them and gradually left them trailing far behind.

A while later the Grand Duke impatiently stuck his head out again. Before him the road was crossed by a tremendous ravine. The gap was spanned by a very narrow wooden bridge. The border.

"Stop!" shouted the Grand Duke. "Stop, fool!"

The team clattered over the planks as the coach dragged to a stop in the middle of the bridge. The driver climbed down from his seat.

"What's the matter with you?" demanded the Grand Duke. "Dolt! Idiot! I don't want to cross the border."

"Oh, forgive me, Your Excellency," the coachman called. He was rapidly doing something to the horses. "I had no intention that you should cross the border, Your Excellency. I just wanted to make sure that your guards don't."

The coachman finished unhitching the team and stepped back, turning to the Grand Duke. "And I might add," he said, as he pulled his muffler completely down from his face, "that you should be more courteous when you speak to the rabbi of Klennitz."

"The rabbi of Klennitz!" The Grand Duke's face changed to a lovely purple, and his eyes bulged to pop out any second.

"Farewell, Your Excellency," called the rabbi, with a flourish of his hand. "I thank you for the escort and fresh horses, and for letting me get ahead of your men; you were most kind. Or rather, I should say, I thank G-d. May you treat my people as well. But have no fear — I shall be back. G-d has never forsaken my people — neither will I!" And with that the rabbi of Klennitz climbed upon one of the lead horses, and the team galloped away.

The four guards now came pounding onto the scene. The Grand Duke forced his huge bulk part way out of the door and screamed: "Guards! Guards! Get him! That's the rabbi of Klennitz!" The guards drew their swords, but of course it was impossible to squeeze past the coach. The Grand Duke leaned out further, still screaming: "Blast you! Don't let the swine escape!" and he exploded into a fit of coughing. He lost his grip and fell. The tyrant hit the rail of the bridge with a heavy impact, and tumbled over. He was still coughing.

At the bottom of the ravine, hundreds of feet below, rushed a raging river. No doubt about it — from now on things were going to be a lot better in the Grand Duke's province.

The Three Questions

One of the forefathers of the Chasam Sofer *was Rabbi Yosef Shmuel of Frankfurt. This is a true story of how he became rabbi of Frankfurt.*

by Dr. Gershon Kranzler

The room where the elders of the Jewish community of Frankfurt were gathered was crowded, but there was no noise. Sadness filled the room like a heavy cloud. Upstairs, in the bedroom, the great and honored rabbi of Frankfurt, Yeshaya Hurwitz, lay dying. The doctors had given up all hope.

As they sat there, trying to imagine Frankfurt without their revered rabbi, the door opened and an attendant motioned to three of the most learned elders to follow him.

"The rabbi wishes to speak to you."

Upstairs, the rabbi rose weakly on his elbows and spoke quietly.

"I know that you are worried about the choice of my successor. I, too, have thought about it, and I want to help you. I will tell you three difficult questions concerning Jewish law. Go out into the world — and whoever can answer the three questions properly should be chosen as my successor." Not long afterward, the rabbi died.

After the month of mourning, the three men left to fulfill their mission. They spent many months on the road, traveling from yeshivah to yeshivah, from country to country — but without success. Finally, they reached the city of Cracow in Poland — a city famous for its great *talmidei chachomim* (Torah scholars). The three men from Frankfurt prayed that they should at last find someone in Cracow great enough to be a worthy successor to their departed rabbi. The Jews of Cracow were greatly honored by the visit of these distinguished men from

Frankfurt and they paid them the highest respect.

So it happened that when one of the richest members of the community celebrated the *Bris Milah* (circumcision) of his newly born son, he invited the distinguished guests to grace his table with their presence. Now, it was customary at a *Bris Milah* for an older brother (if there was one) of the newly arrived baby to say a *drashah,* a little speech about a point in Jewish law, for the assembled guests. Of course, the young boy did not make up the *drashah* himself — after all, he was only twelve years old — but he was able to repeat the *drashah* his teacher had taught him.

The little boy — David was his name — was nervous at first, but he soon settled down and explained his point very clearly. And wonder of wonders! Imagine how surprised the three men from Frankfurt were when they realized that in his speech the young boy had answered every one of the three questions of their test! They could hardly believe their ears! Had their prayers really been answered so soon?

As soon as David finished, the eldest of the three men hurried up to the proud father.

"Where is the teacher of your son, David?" he asked excitedly. "We must see him at once!"

"Why, of course," the father said, and he led the three men to the little *shul* called "*Chavuras Shomrim Laboker.*" There he pointed out to them a young man sitting in a corner next to a glowing pot-bellied stove.

"That is Rabbi Yosef Shmuel," he said. "He is the *shammos* (caretaker) in this *shul* and he also teaches the children during the day."

The three men walked over to him and saw that he was eagerly studying.

"Would you excuse us for a moment?" they began.

"I'm sorry, but I cannot interrupt my studies. There is so much to learn … so much to learn … and I have so little time."

"But we must speak with you. It is of the greatest importance."

"Well, if you must — see me during twilight."

The three men had no choice. In the evening they returned and spoke to Rabbi Yosef Shmuel. They told him about their mission, about the three questions and about David's *drashah* at the *Bris Milah*.

"We invite you to accept the position of rabbi in Frankfurt — because you are the only man worthy to succeed our revered Rabbi, may he rest in peace."

Rabbi Yosef Shmuel thought for a moment and then spoke.

"My dear friends, believe me when I say that I am very honored by your request. However, you must also believe me when I say that I am not worthy enough to accept this high position. I do not think I should leave my task of teaching young children the holy words of our Torah. I cannot accept your offer."

The three men pleaded with him, they argued, they tried to

convince him — but nothing would help. He would not leave Cracow. Now the three men were especially disappointed, for they had seen in his answer the kind of earnestness and sincerity they wanted in their future rabbi. But they had to leave Cracow without Rabbi Yosef Shmuel.

And now a remarkable thing happened. As soon as the coach carrying the three men for Frankfurt left Cracow, Rabbi Yosef Shmuel took sick. With every passing day his illness became ever more serious. The doctors were puzzled. They could find no cause for his sickness — nor could they find a cure.

A few more days and Rabbi Yosef Shmuel was near death. His friends had already gathered and were praying for him. Then suddenly, he raised his head and said in a loud voice: "Oh L-rd, if you really insist that I leave my students and become the rabbi of Frankfurt — I agree!"

And just as suddenly as it came, his sickness now began to leave him. He slowly began to regain his strength and was on the way to complete recovery.

As soon as his friends heard his willingness to accept the position in Frankfurt, the leaders of the Cracow community sent messengers in all directions to find the three men. And the messengers, too, were in for a surprise! For they found the three men in an inn not more than five miles from Cracow! It turned out that their coach had suffered an accident, one of the men from Frankfurt had broken his arm and couldn't continue the trip until it had at least partially healed.

Naturally, they were overjoyed to hear of the miracle that caused Rabbi Yosef Shmuel to change his mind. They returned to Cracow and made the preparations to bring their new rabbi to Frankfurt.

In Frankfurt, Rabbi Yosef Shmuel devoted all his time to the study of Torah. It is said that he learned through the entire Talmud forty-two times to fulfill the command of ... וְדִבַּרְתָּ בָּם ..., "... and you should speak of them ..." (*Dvorim* 6:7) because בָּם has a numerical value of 42. He wrote many books and commentaries and was one of the guiding lights of the Jewish people.

A Bag Full of Hope

Adapted by Rochel Feder

Yankel Zeldas was always happy with what he had, as long as he was able to earn his living honestly. He would buy fresh fruits and vegetables in the small villages and then sell them in the big city of Leipzig at a small profit. He worked hard and earned little, but he and his wife were always content.

One morning as Yankel was on his way to a nearby village, he noticed a mail wagon passing by, its back doors flung wide open. He called out to the driver to stop, but the driver did not hear him, and suddenly a big bundle of mail fell off the wagon. Yankel ran after the wagon shouting, "Stop! Stop! You lost something!", but the driver rode on, unaware of what had happened.

Yankel bent down to pick up the bag. He was suddenly filled with a terrible desire to open some of the letters in the pack. A voice inside him said: *"Yankel, what's gotten into you? That mail doesn't belong to you! Hurry up and return it!"*

Still, Yankel thought, "I'll just take a little peek and then I'll give it back."

He opened one envelope, but there was nothing interesting inside it. He then opened a second envelope and in this one he was astonished to find an enormous sum of money.

Again the little voice within him spoke up: *"See that, Yankel? Why did you have to open these envelopes? What's inside is none of your business. Next you'll start thinking what you'll do with all that money, and thoughts like that are not going to do you any good!"*

Yankel stood there, lost in thought. "How wonderful it would be if this money were indeed mine! All my life I've worked so hard. With this money I'd be rich!"

Yankel's wife, Tzipporah, was on her hands and knees, scrubbing the kitchen floor, when he walked in. His heart leaped with joy as he imagined her reaction to their new-found riches. For a moment he stood in the doorway, watching her as she worked. "Things will be different from now on," he thought happily, looking down at her tired face and chapped red hands, so worn from all the years of scrubbing and washing. "My Tzipporah won't ever scrub a floor again. She'll be a grand lady from now on."

Yankel told his wife of his great fortune and waited for her delighted reaction. She opened her eyes widely and asked, "What's gotten into you, Yankel? Have you gone mad? The money isn't ours. You must return it!"

"Tzipporah," he reasoned, "listen to me. This is not stealing. I found the money and I'm keeping it. That's all."

Tzipporah was a stubborn woman. "Yankel," she pleaded, "all

your life you have been such an honest man. I never heard a lie come from your mouth, nor did you ever take a penny that wasn't yours. How many times have I heard you say that we mustn't owe the grocer money for even a day because he, too, must pay his bills, because his children also need shoes? What has come over you? Don't you realize what you're doing?"

"Tell me, Tzipporah, have I ever told you to do something wrong? Why can't you trust me now? Imagine how different things can be if we keep this money! Don't you think I realize that you must be ashamed to always wear the same old dress to shul every *Shabbos?* Now you will be able to buy yourself beautiful clothes. No more scrubbing floors. From now on we will eat meat every day, and you and the children will be healthy and strong. Not only will life be better for us, Tzipporah, but we will never forget that we were once poor. We will give generously to the needy and do much good with our money."

Tzipporah would not listen. She wept and pleaded with her husband, and tried to make him understand that he was wrong, yet Yankel still insisted on keeping the money.

When he returned the other letters to the post office, he was told that an envelope full of money was reported missing, and was it not among the others? Yankel made believe that he knew nothing about it. He realized that the police might suspect him of taking the money, since he had found the other letters. So he took the money and hid it carefully, just in case they would decide to search his house.

Sure enough, one night, when Yankel was eating supper, he was interrupted by a loud knocking on the door. Tzipporah went to open the door. Her face turned white when she saw that the police had come. The chief inspector stepped forward and with a stern expression on his face announced the purpose of his visit. "I am sorry to tell you this, sir, but we have reason to suspect you of having the missing money, since you were the one who found the bundle of mail which contained the envelope with the money inside. We have come to search your home."

The police searched the house thoroughly, but the money was not to be found. All the while, Tzipporah sat at the table, wringing her hands, her face pale, her heart pounding in fear. When the police finally left, she was at first unable to speak. After a few minutes, she recovered from the terrifying ordeal. She turned to her husband and she spoke to him a calm voice.

"Yankel, I know you mean well. I know that it is mostly for me and for the children that you want the money, because you want to make us happy. But you cannot make us happy this way. My father was a simple person, but he always tried to do what was right. It would have hurt him terribly if he would have known that I have money that does not belong to me." She paused for a moment and then went on. "We *cannot* keep the money, Yankel," she whispered. "You know yourself, deep down, that it's not right!"

Yankel sat there, his head bent, deep in thought. At last, in a voice that trembled with emotion, he spoke. "You are right, I wanted the best for you, but we have no right to keep it. We will return the money."

❀ ❀ ❀

It was late at night. Rabbi Baruch Frankel-Thumim of Leipzig, Germany, was one of the greatest *gaonim* (Torah geniuses) of his time (about a hundred-fifty years ago). He was the father-in-law of the famous Sanzer *Rav*, Rabbi Chaim Halberstam. Reb Baruch sat in his study, deeply engrossed in Torah study. It was a warm night and the window was open. Suddenly, a small package flew in through the window and fell to the floor. Reb Baruch looked up, surprised.

"What can this be?" he wondered. He opened the package and he immediately realized that this was the missing money that everybody in town was discussing.

"Probably," he thought, "the person who took it is sorry now and wants to return it, but he doesn't dare return it to the police for then everybody will know that he is the thief. Surely, the money was thrown in to me, so I should give it back."

He ran to the door, hoping to catch a glimpse of the person who had thrown it in. But Tzipporah, good honest Tzipporah, was not to be seen.

"Nobody will know now. Nobody," she thought as she hurried back to her simple little home, feeling tremendously relieved.

Now Reb Baruch had a problem on his hands. If he would give the money back to the police, the first thing they would ask him would be, "How'd you get it?" They would never believe that somebody just threw it in his window. They would say that he was covering up for someone, that he knew who took the money, but did not want to tell who it was. "What can I do?", he wondered.

Reb Baruch was acquainted with a local priest, and he decided to use his help in solving the problem. After telling him about the money and how it fell into his hands, Reb Baruch asked, "Tell me, when someone comes to you and confesses his guilt in connection with some crime, do you have to tell the police about it?"

"No, Rabbi Frankel," answered the priest. "I am not obligated to tell the police anything. All confessions are strictly confidential. Why do you ask?"

"I'll tell you why," said Reb Baruch. "You can do me a big favor if you give the money to the police. They would not ask you any questions!"

The priest readily agreed to do so.

The police were relieved to recover the money and the priest was given a handsome reward. However, he felt that Reb Baruch deserved the reward and turned it over to him.

Reb Baruch refused. "I do not deserve this money any more than you do." He paused for a minute, deep in thought. Then he smiled: "That poor man, Yankel Zeldas, is the one who deserves the reward. The police suspected him and searched his house, causing him much anxiety and shame. He is the one who should get the reward."

And so it was. Yankel Zeldas got the reward. He used the money to start a little business. Gradually, the business grew, until he became a very wealthy man, much wealthier than he would have been had he kept the lost money. He became rich in an honest way ... because he listened to the voice of his conscience, and the voice of his honest wife, Tzipporah.

Yossel, the Tailor

by Rabbi Bernard Goldenberg

Yossel, the tailor, slouched in his seat, a deep frown on his face. All around him people sat enraptured as they listened attentively to the rabbi's *drashah* (sermon) on *Shabbos Hagadol* (the *Shabbos* before *Pesach*), for the speaker was Prague's new chief rabbi, Yechezkel Landau. And the people who listened to him in the Great Synagogue showed very clearly that they were very proud of their famous new rabbi.

But not so Yossel, the tailor.

He snickered and made funny faces. And by this he wanted to show his neighbors to the right and his neighbors to the left that, to him at least, the rabbi of Prague was "not such a great man." They, the neighbors, as well as all the other Jews in Prague, were proud that they had as their new leader a man of such Torah learning as Rabbi Yechezkel Landau. How hard they had worked to get him! But not so Yossel. To Yossel the rabbi was not good enough as a leader — not great enough — not deep enough as a scholar.

Not that Yossel was such a *talmid chacham* (Torah scholar) himself. It was just a strange quirk in Yossel's personality. He just found something wrong with all the rabbi's actions, speeches or learning. No matter what the rabbi did, Yossel was sure to complain.

Rabbi Landau finished his sermon, kissed the *poroches* (curtain) of the *Aron Kodesh,* and walked down to his seat. Almost immediately there was a hubbub of noise and a buzz of whispered talk. All the people were commenting on the rabbi's wonderful sermon. This one liked the rabbi's learning, the other one liked his way of speaking, the third one liked the rabbi's personality.

But while all this was going on, what was Yossel, the tailor, doing?

Yossel was running from group to group. He would approach each group, cocking an ear to one side so as to hear better. If the conversation was about the speech, Yossel would immediately elbow his way to the center of the group and begin to criticize the rabbi.

If someone would say, "The rabbi showed us today how much wisdom he possesses," Yossel would interrupt and say, "You call that wisdom?" If someone would comment about the rabbi's knowledge of the *Talmud,* Yossel would gruffly exclaim, "Ha, what does he know of the *Talmud?*"

No matter what compliment was paid to the rabbi, Yossel would immediately oppose it. From group to group he walked and from group to group he spread his criticism of the rabbi. No one dared interrupt him, for Yossel wouldn't allow that. And no one could outshout him, for Yossel had a voice as deep as a foghorn. His voice could easily drown out anyone else's in Prague.

Yossel had never been like this. Never before, in all his days in Prague, did Yossel ever bellow or shout so much. He was a simple man who barely made a living from his tailor-shop. In the synagogue, he would sit where all the poor people sat — on the last bench in the back; and seldom, if ever, did he raise his voice. He never complained about anyone, nor did anyone ever complain about him. And then boom! All of a sudden Yossel, the quiet, modest tailor, became a man of violent opinion and loud voice. And only when it concerned the rabbi. At all other times he was still the same quiet Yossel.

Of course, the "big shots" in town disregarded Yossel's speeches against the rabbi. "After all," they said, "who is Yossel? A simple tailor who doesn't know anything. Why worry about his opinions? Who listens to him anyway?"

But not so Rabbi Yechezkel Landau. He did listen, and he did worry. For he loved all the Jews in town — rich man, poor man, learned man, ignorant man. They were all Jews, weren't they? And so when he heard that a member of his community was finding fault with him, the rabbi became worried. "Even if he is a tailor," thought the rabbi, "perhaps the man has some reason." And so Reb Yechezkel Landau, the chief rabbi of Prague, called in his *shammos* (caretaker) and asked him to fetch Yossel, the tailor.

This was the moment Yossel feared. He was afraid to walk to the rabbi's house. But there was the rabbi's *shammos* walking alongside of him. And every now and then he gently prodded Yossel along. He, Yossel, was afraid to open the door to the rabbi's house. But the door was opened for him. And now Yossel, the tailor, was face to face with the chief rabbi of Prague, the rabbi of thousands of Jews.

There was an open *Gemara* on the table. And before it sat the rabbi. He lifted his head and Yossel began trembling in his boots. A deep sigh escaped the rabbi and Yossel almost fainted. Soon a tender smile crossed the rabbi's face and, very kindly and gently, he asked Yossel to sit down alongside of him.

"I heard," said the rabbi, "that you find fault with me. Please tell me what faults I have, and I surely will try to correct them."

"I …" stammered Yossel, "faults, Rabbi?" His voice trailed off.

"Then people lie when they tell me these stories about you?" the rabbi asked.

"Oh, no," Yossel exclaimed, finally gaining courage. "It's true, It's true what people say. I do criticize you constantly, and I'll even tell you why." Then in a shouting voice Yossel, the tailor, began to tell why he became the rabbi's violent opponent.

According to Yossel, it all started when Rabbi Landau became Prague's chief rabbi. As befit such a great man, the town declared a holiday on the day he was scheduled to arrive in the city. On the appointed day everyone in Prague was outside of the city limits waiting impatiently for the rabbi's arrival. Plans were ready for a big reception.

Finally, they saw a simple coach in the distance. And as the coach came near, the crowd saw that its lone passenger was their new chief rabbi.

Then, the ceremonies began. The president of the Jewish community stepped forward, welcomed the rabbi to Prague, and introduced himself. Then the other rabbis of Prague introduced themselves. Then came the *gabbaim* of the synagogue, the judges, the rich men, the elders and the wise men. It took a long time, but the new chief rabbi met them all and learned their names.

Yossel was also in that throng of people. Did he know that the new chief rabbi was there? Yes, he did. *But* — did the new rabbi know that Yossel was there? Why, of course not. For he was not among those introduced. He was neither rich nor wise, neither clever nor learned. He was just a tailor — Yossel. And the new rabbi did not know Yossel — not even his name.

"Right then and there," Yossel continued, "I decided that the new chief rabbi — and the town too — should know that there is a tailor in town, and that this tailor's name is Yossel. And so to gain this attention, I fell upon this plan. I decided to constantly criticize the rabbi. Now

everyone in town knows Yossel the tailor. Even the rabbi. For," Yossel finished truimphantly, "did you not send for me because you too heard of Yossel, the tailor?"

Yossel lowered his eyes. The rabbi was silent. The room was silent. It seemed as if the whole world was still and waiting.

Rabbi Yechezkel Landau knitted his brows once, twice, then passed his left hand over his beard. "You know, Yossel," he began, "there are two ways of getting what you want. A bad way and a good way. You wanted fame. You wanted people to hear of Yossel, the tailor. You chose the bad way. You found fault where no fault existed. You lied, you sinned.

"But, there is another way. And it will get you there just the same. And you will not have to sin against *Hashem*. Do that, and *Hashem* will forgive you.

"In a few days, I, the chief rabbi of Prague, will come to your tailor shop. What will I want? I will want you to make for me a good coat for

Shabbos wear. I will pay you for it. All you have to do is to make for me a coat that will be handsome and neat, and everyone will know of Yossel, the tailor. For everyone will then know that the rabbi's *Shabbos* coat was made by none other than Yossel. Which Yossel? Yossel, the tailor!"

And so it was.

On a *Shabbos* a few weeks later, Rabbi Landau came to Prague's Great Synagogue. He walked down the aisle wearing his new *Shabbos* coat. Everyone in the synagogue (and the synagogue was packed with Prague's most important people) was abuzz with excitement. "Did you see the rabbi's new *Shabbos* coat?" "Who made it?" "Why, don't you know? Yossel, the tailor."

Yossel sat in the back and smiled. Everyone knew Yossel. He was happy. For this time he reached his goal in the right way. Was he not famous now as Yossel, the tailor, the man who made Rabbi Yechezkel Landau's new coat?

The Clever Answer

A true story adapted by Ben Gerson

Rabbi Yonoson Eibeschutz, the chief rabbi of the Lorraine Province in Germany, was beloved by all. Everyone loved him for his kindness and good deeds, and everyone respected him for his wisdom, intelligence, and sharp mind. Truly he was a great *talmid chacham* (Torah scholar) and a leader of the Jewish community. And thus it became a common occurrence that when a little Jewish baby was born, people didn't say to the proud parents *"mazel tov, mazel tov,"* and leave it at that — they added a complete new sentence which went something like this: *"Mazel tov, mazel tov.* May your son grow up to be another Reb Yonoson Eibeschutz" and then the parents would gently close their eyes for a minute and answer sincerely, *"Amen, amen,* let us hope so."

And it wasn't only the Jewish people who loved their rabbi. The non-Jewish people, too, loved Reb Yonoson Eibeschutz. It was customary to compliment a very bright person by saying "Ah, he has a head like Rabbi Yonoson," or ""Let us ask him; he has almost as much understanding as Reb Yonoson."

And so, everybody — Jew and non-Jew — respected the wise and kind scholar. They would bring him all their disputes, arguments and questions, and Reb Yonoson would always solve their problems and help them in their troubles. Yes, Reb Yonoson was popular and beloved by everyone. Well — not really by *everyone.* There was one man who had always hated Reb Yonoson.

This man (who was well-known for his harsh treatment of his servants and subjects) was none other than the ruler of the province himself, the Duke of Lorraine.

Hardly a week passed that the Duke wouldn't call Reb Yonoson to his palace. There was always some pretense. One time he wanted to test the rabbi's remarkable memory; the next time his intelligence. Once he asked him to play chess against the champion of all Europe. The next time it was to solve a mathematical puzzle that had baffled all the university professors. And as Reb Yonoson always knew the right answers, the Duke's hatred knew no bounds.

One day the rabbi was sitting in the *beis hamidrash* studying the *Talmud.* Suddenly, the door flew open violently and three of the leading Jews of Metz came in crying and sobbing. *"Rebbi, Rebbi,"* they cried, "All the Jews must leave the Duchy of Lorraine by sunset. The Duke just signed the order, and his messenger has just announced his edict."

Without another word the rabbi put on his coat and hurried down to the Duke's palace. As he entered, Reb Yonoson saw a sly smile on the Duke's face. "The Duke must have arranged something really sinister to issue such a severe edict," thought Reb Yonoson to himself, "but let's see what is what. After all we have *Hashem* on our side."

"What is this sudden order to expel the Jews from your province, Your Excellency?" quietly asked Rabbi Yonoson Eibeschutz. "Is it fair to force people who have lived here for years to become wanderers in a few hours?"

"Well," replied the Duke slowly, obviously enjoying this moment of triumph over the cleverest Jew in the Province, "I don't know whether it is fair or not, but I do know that I am merely fullfilling a prophecy which I have found written in one of the old history books of this duchy. You see, my dear rabbi," he continued, "perhaps I am not as clever as you are, but I certainly deem it my privilege to do what our history books have said would most certainly come about."

"Well," replied Rabbi Yonoson a little hastily, "what is it then that is found in your old history books?"

"Nothing much," replied the Duke, "merely a sentence about the Jews. Something that reads like this: 'A terrible event is coming, the likes of which the world has never seen till this day.' Now, you see rabbi, I am not bad, I am merely fulfilling a prophecy. Oh, by the way, how many letters are there in the prophecy of the old history book I just mentioned?"

"Sixty-eight," replied Rabbi Yonoson almost immediately, for so marvelous was his memory.

"And the number of words?" continued the Duke, as if to hurt the rabbi.

"Seventeen. Precisely the number of letters found in the Hebrew sentence: *Am Yisroel chai l'olmei ad* — the people of Israel will live forever." The Duke was truly amazed at the rabbi's quick and sure memory. Suddenly he smiled. "Tell me, would you like to do away with my edict that expels all the Jews from my province?"

"Yes of course," answered the rabbi. "What are your conditions?"

"Very simple," continued the Duke. "Tell me, just how many Jews are there in my state?" Reb Yonoson replied, "45,760."

"If so," said the Duke, "then here is what you should do and you'll be able to save your people. In an hour my edict against the Jews is to go into effect. Before that hour you must come back with a piece of parchment no bigger than the piece on which your people ordinarily write their *mezuzah*. On that piece of parchment you will write the sentence you just mentioned, forty-five thousand … eh, eh, how many Jews do you say there are in this duchy?"

"I said 45,760."

"If before that hour you can write out on an ordinary *mezuzah* parchment — 45,760 times — the sentence about the people of Israel you just mentioned, I will definitely tear up the order expelling the Jews."

Rabbi Yonoson's face looked deeply worried. What a responsibility the Duke put on him. Suddenly he smiled, turned to the Duke and said, "Please G-d, I will be back in less than an hour."

In less that an hour, Reb Yonoson showed the Duke a parchment with the following written on it:

The Duke looked and frowned. "What is this?" he shouted. "Are you laughing at me? What is this paper you brought here?"

"Just what you requested, Your Majesty. 45,760 times the sentence עַם יִשְׂרָאֵל חַי לְעוֹלְמֵי עַד. Begin with the big ע in the center, go in each direction and you'll find that there are 45,760 complete Hebrew sentences there."

The Duke looked. He didn't understand it yet completely. But he instinctively knew that Rabbi Yonoson had outsmarted him and defeated him once again. The edict was torn up.

A half year later there was a big tumult in the rabbi's house. The Duke's carriage was outside. Out came the Duke and in he walked to Rabbi Yonoson's private study.

"Rabbi," he said immediately upon entering, "Happy is the people that has such leaders. I just finished reading the parchment. Yes, it is true. The sentence is found there 45,760 times."

The Tycoon With the Broom

by Rabbi Zevulun Weisberger

Mr. Morris Berger, President of Berger Plastics Inc., had just left his office. The owner of one of the most successful firms in its field did not leave unnoticed. Two of his employees, Daniel Powers and Brian Winter, were watching him intently.

"There he goes again, two o'clock on the dot," Brian Winter whispered, "with that brown package under his arm. I wonder what is in it?"

"And, most of all, where does he go?" wondered Powers thoughtfully. "It's so strange — every week, the same time!"

"And he always comes back perspiring, but happy and content, just as if he had completed another million dollar deal," remarked Winter.

"Let's ask his secretary, Miss Neuman. Maybe she will tell us."

"Miss Neuman, we have a question," Powers said as they approached her, "where does the boss go every Friday afternoon at two o'clock?"

"Yes, and what's in that brown package he always takes along?" asked Winter.

Miss Neuman seemed surprised at the questions, but, with a sly smile, she remarked, "Tsk, Tsk, gentlemen, don't you know — curiosity killed the cat!"

"Oh, is it some international secret?" Powers countered, raising his eyebrows in false surprise. The men smiled and left the office.

"Looks like she's not talking," Brian Winter said.

"Well, I have an idea," Powers replied. "He always brings the package back with him when he returns. Let's distract him for a while and examine the package."

"How do you propose to do it?"

"Well, when the boss returns, you ask him if he could look at your latest research report on the new product. Meanwhile, I'll slip into the office, open the package and grab a look."

"How about Miss Neuman?"

"I'll have to arrange for her to have a telephone call, a long one — from my wife."

And so the grand scheme was hatched. Little did Powers know where his plan would land him.

Berger returned at four o'clock, almost time for closing. Everything started to work according to plan. Mr. Berger was examining the papers on Winter's desk, Miss Neuman got her long call, and Powers slipped into the open office. He went straight to the closet and found the package. He opened it ...

"Well, did you find out what was in the package?" Winter asked Powers when they met late that afternoon.

"Sure, but wait till you hear this — you would never, in a million years, guess what it is ... overalls and a work-shirt!"

"You must be kidding — what would he be doing with work clothes?"

"Sure is queer — maybe he robs banks in his spare time."

"I'm getting more curious by the minute — now we *must* find out what he does."

"Well, there is only one way to do it — follow him and see."

"OK — it's a deal — next Friday!"

They agreed that Powers would follow Mr. Berger while Winter would cover for him in the office in case any questions were asked.

Two o'clock came and Morris Berger left his office. Powers slipped out by another door. He watched Berger leave the building and cross the street, turn the corner and walk down the block. Powers kept him in sight, carefully concealing himself to avoid detection.

Two blocks later, Mr. Berger neared the synagogue on Greenleaf Street. He unlocked the door and entered. The synagogue! What would he be doing there on a Friday afternoon? Perhaps he only stopped in to pick up something. Powers waited impatiently outside.

But Mr. Berger did not come out. Perhaps the secret work was going on inside the synagogue? Powers walked around the building looking for an unlocked window. Little did he know that a woman across the street saw him and suspected him of being a burglar trying to break in.

Powers found a window that was slightly open and peered into the sanctuary. He heard someone moving around inside.

Suddenly, he was startled by the wailing sirens of a police car. Brakes screeched and Powers turned to find three policemen facing him with guns drawn.

"HANDS UP!" they shouted, "we have you covered!"

Powers was astounded. What was this all about?

"What's the matter, officers?" he asked, "what did I do?"

"Isn't it obvious — trying to break into the synagogue — that's what! A woman across the street was watching you prowling, and now we saw you at that window."

"But I wasn't trying to go in — honest — I was just looking for someone."

Sergeant O'Reilly handcuffed him saying, "I know — that's what they all say. You were probably looking for a lost cat — or was it a dog?"

"Please, officer, look inside the building. My boss is in there! You're arresting an innocent man."

"Okay, buddy, we'll search the building and see what we find."

The alert on the police radio was picked up by the local newspaper. They dispatched a reporter to the scene and alerted Alan Meyers, the synagogue president. Meyers rushed over to investigate.

O'Reilly and his men knocked at the door. After several minutes, it opened. There, dressed in overalls and a dirty workshirt with a broom in his hand, was Mr. Morris Berger, President of Berger Plastics Inc., and one of the wealthiest Jews in America. Sergeant O'Reilly almost fainted.

"Mr. Berger," he exclaimed, "what are you, of all people, doing here in that getup?"

Mr. Berger was very surprised to see the police. He regained his composure to say, "Oh, come in, gentlemen. What seems to be the trouble?"

Pointing to Powers, O'Reilly said, "We caught this fellow snooping around the building. He claims he works for you. Do you know him?"

"Powers!" he exclaimed, "what are you doing here?"

Sheepishly, Powers explained that his curiosity had gotten the better of him.

Mr. Berger smiled, "Oh, well, no harm done. I guess these gentlemen are also wondering. And I see Mr. Meyers coming. All of you are waiting to hear my story."

"Yes, if you don't mind, sir. We have to file a report," said O'Reilly.

"Mr. Berger!" Mr. Meyers exclaimed, "what are you doing with that broom — and with those clothes?"

It's really very simple," Mr. Berger replied, smiling. "What does anyone do with a broom — he sweeps the floor!"

"But, Mr. Berger," Sergeant O'Reilly protested, "you can afford to hire a million workers — why do you have to do it yourself?"

"That's right," Mr. Meyers chimed in. "We have a custodian — that's his job."

"Well, you see, gentlemen, *Shabbos* is about to arrive and the synagogue should look its best in honor of the *Shabbos* Queen's arrival. When a queen arrives, she has to find a sparkling, beautiful home awaiting her. Our Sages tell us that everyone should help prepare for *Shabbos.* This is my way of doing it — and my dirty shirt and trousers are the uniform of my service to the queen.

"But why the synagogue, Mr. Berger?" Sergeant O'Reilly asked, "why not do this in your own home. Isn't it the Sabbath there, too?"

"It sure is, but my family has the situation very much under control. Evelyn and our sons and daughters do all the work themselves. They hardly let the maid lift a finger to make *Shabbos* preparations. They do it so well, there is nothing left for me. I had to look for another place to be involved — and what could be better than the *shul?*"

"And to think I was going to recommend a raise for our custodian at the next Board meeting — I thought that he had done such a good job," Mr. Meyers remarked, shaking his head in disbelief.

The next day there were pictures on the front pages of the local papers of "The Tycoon with the Broom."

Everyone got some unexpected publicity — Mr. Berger, Powers, the *shul,* and most of all — *Shabbos Kodesh!* (Oops, I forgot to tell you what happened to Powers. Well, of course, the police let that red-faced man go and Mr. Berger laughed the whole thing off. Powers learned a few things, though — about the dangers of curiosity and the holiness of *Shabbos.)*

The Story-Teller and the Bishop

A true story retold by Rabbi Beryl Merling

About 100 years ago, in a small Bavarian inn, at one of the tables in the corner, sat three men. One of them, an elderly man, about sixty, was Reb Zelig who had been the *shammos* or personal attendant, of the *Baal Shem* of Michelstadt. After the *Baal Shem* had died, Reb Zelig became a story-teller, traveling from city to city, telling stories from the life of the *Baal Shem*. The other two were Jewish merchants from Italy. The three of them had just met by chance in this inn. The two merchants had been sitting for hours now, listening to Reb Zelig's wonderful tales.

Finally, one of them said, "Reb Zelig, I think you would be interested to know that in the city of Venice there lives a certain banker, Giuseppe Menashe. He is a very rich and noble Jew and is greatly respected in his community. Now this Giuseppe has announced that he will give a golden ducat to anyone who can tell him a story about the *Baal Shem* of Michelstadt. Why don't you go to Venice, Reb Zelig, and see this man? With all your stories about the *Baal Shem* you would make a fortune! You could go there just once and retire for the rest of your life!"

This sounded very logical to Reb Zelig but it took him some time to make up his mind, because, old and tired as he was, he didn't care to travel so far away from his home. But he finally decided to go and after three weeks of difficult traveling, he reached Venice.

This was on a Tuesday. The next day, Reb Zelig was taken to Giuseppe Menashe. Reb Zelig saw before him a man, about fifty years old, with a long striking beard that already was beginning to show hairs of gray. Signor Menashe, for this is how he was called in Venice, made a good impression on Reb Zelig. He seemed to inspire confidence and he received Reb Zelig very kindly.

"What do you want, my good man?" he asked Reb Zelig.

"I was a student and close friend of the *Baal Shem* of Michelstadt and I heard that you are very interested in the life and deeds of my great rabbi."

Signor Menashe seemed very happy when he heard this.

"Yes, yes, indeed! I'm really very sorry that I cannot spent more time with you right now. You see, I am a very busy man here — my bank, you know. But please remain here over *Shabbos* as my guest and then we shall have more time to talk at leisure about the great *Baal Shem.* I assure you — you shall have a very pleasant time while you stay with us."

Reb Zelig consented and moved into the beautiful house of Signor Menashe. A beautiful house — as befitted a very wealthy man. Reb Zelig was given a fine room and was treated with the greatest honor and respect.

Friday night, after the meal, Signor Menashe sat back and said with an expectant smile, "And now we shall hear what we have waited for so long."

Reb Zelig stroked his forehead wondering which of his many stories to tell. Signor Menashe and his family and the other guests at the table waited. They waited three minutes, five minutes, ten — but Reb Zelig did not start yet. He became slightly embarrassed and began to sweat. He rubbed his forehead again and again — but instead of deciding *which* story to tell, Reb Zelig *could not remember a single story!* This was awful. It has never happened before. His mind was a complete blank! A half-hour went by and still no story. The family and guests began to grumble — Impostor! Cheat!

But the kind Signor Menashe quieted them. "Reb Zelig, do not be disturbed. You must be tired from your long journey. Tomorrow, when you are rested, we shall hear some stories from you."

Reb Zelig was relieved — but not for long — because on *Shabbos* morning — no stories! Again, Signor Menashe was gracious and said "We shall wait until tonight, at the *Melaveh Malkeh.*"

Then, when it happened for a third time, Reb Zelig was really worried. He did not know what to think!

He went to his host and said, "Please forgive me, Signor Menashe, but I cannot explains this strange occurrence. Perhaps I should never have come to Venice. But it is really strange — I cannot even see the *Baal Shem* in my mind's eye! I must thank you for your hospitality. I shall leave tomorrow."

"No, no, Reb Zelig, don't leave. Stay a few days longer. I am still very anxious to hear your stories. Maybe you'll remember in a few days."

Reb Zelig agreed to remain overnight. The following morning he said to Signor Menashe, "All night I have not slept, trying to remember a story, all in vain. I really must go ... But wait! I remember! Just now I reminded myself of something. Would you like to hear it?"

Reb Zelig began, "This was about twenty years ago. One day, the *Baal Shem* called to me and said, 'Prepare yourself for a trip. We both must go to Donbirn in the Tyrol, for the Easter festival!' I was very surprised, for no Jews were allowed to stay in the Tyrol without special permission. What could the *Baal Shem* have wanted there?

"When we arrived in Dornbirn, however, we found that one Jewish family had received permission to live there. They were unwilling for us to stay with them, especially because it was the time of the Easter festival, which was to be held in the town square, directly opposite their house, and it was dangerous for us to be seen at that time. But the *Baal Shem* insisted and they finally agreed.

"A large platform had been set up in the square and Sunday morning — Easter — the *Baal Shem* and I watched a gathering crowd from behind a curtained window. At ten o'clock the bishop arrived.

"At that moment the *Baal Shem* spoke to me. 'Go up to the bishop and whisper in his ear that the *Baal Shem* of Michelstadt is here and wants to speak to him.' I was astounded but did not question my rabbi. I walked out into the crowd, my heart beating fearfully, and delivered the message.

"The bishop looked at me for a second and whispered back, 'After I finish the service.' I returned his answer to the *Baal Shem*. He looked angry and said, 'Go back! Tell him to come immediately! Every second he delays, the danger increases.' We were afraid now that the *Baal Shem* had gone out of his mind, but I had been trained not to question his commands. I delivered the second message and, to my great surprise, the bishop told an assistant to carry on with the service and then followed me. No one could understand the meaning of what was going on.

"Back in the house, the *Baal Shem* asked to be left alone with the bishop. For two hours, they were alone in a room. I do not know what went on there. All I know is that the bishop came out of the room, hurried to his carriage in the square and drove away. That is all I know of the story."

Suddenly Signor Menashe got up and, in a trembling voice, made

the blessing of *"Shehecheyanu"*. He then turned to Reb Zelig.

"Twenty years have I waited for this day! I am, or rather was, the bishop of your story. But let me start from the beginning.

"I was once one of the best pupils of the *Baal Shem*. For four years I learned very well in Michelstadt and everyone had high hopes for me. Then one day, I met by accident (at least, then I thought it was by accident) the priest from Ohrbach. He told me he wanted me to teach him Hebrew. I thought that this was harmless and started to teach him every day. But while I was teaching him, he was also teaching me! Every day he talked to me about his religion — he flattered me about my wonderful mind and my great possibilities — he promised me the best of everything — if only I would accept his beliefs. I was young then and not so wise, and after a few months I consented.

"I left Michelstadt. No one knew what had happened to me. My family and friends thought that I had died in an accident and they mourned for me. But I was alive — in a monastery in Feldkirk. I studied well and soon I became a priest. I was really quite capable and I grew and advanced in the church system until I finally became a bishop. By this time, I was quite rich and I now realize that, consciously or subconsciously, it was because of my greed for money that I enjoyed my position.

"But, little by little, I began to regret my conversion and one day I decided to write to my old rabbi, the *Baal Shem*, to ask him if there was any hope for a sinner like me."

Signor Menashe took a bundle of letters from a locked drawer in his desk.

"This is my total correspondence with the *Baal Shem*. Read the first letter and tell me if a father could write his son a more loving letter. Although I had sinned, he felt that I could still repent. I was sure then that G-d Himself, the Father of Mercy, would also forgive me.

"But it took me a long time to break away — my greed for money and honor was still within me. We wrote many letters back and forth. The *Baal Shem* told me to break away immediately and forbade me to take even a coin of my church-earned wealth. I could not make up my mind.

"Finally, I decided that after the Easter festival in Dornbirn, I would really leave, and I wrote the *Baal Shem* about my decision. He did not answer that letter. Instead he came himself to Dornbirn. He sent you to call me. You remember now that I had to go to him *immediately*. I can tell you what happened in that room! He said that if I didn't break away that very minute, I would never again repent. It was now or never! Even so he wasn't sure that my repentance would be accepted — perhaps only my death could cleanse me.

"I saw that he was right — and did as he told me. I took the name Giuseppe Menashe and have tried to live a proper Jewish live. G-d has helped me and I prospered here.

"But I was never sure that my repentance was really accepted. When you came to Venice, I recognized you, although you didn't recognize me. I knew it was some sign from my dear, departed rabbi. When you couldn't remember a single story, I realized that my repentance had not been enough. All the time you were here, I prayed and learned all through the night. Finally, you told me my own story. I am sure now that my soul is at last clean again. You don't know how happy you have made me!"

Signor Menashe gave Reb Zelig a handsome gift of money from which he could live the rest of his days quietly and peacefully.

And so ends the story of the Bishop and the Story-Teller.